*She heard the note of caring in his voice and it made her blink back tears.*

Drat the man. He had the capacity to get under her skin. And why? Because he was big and handsome and gentle and….

And a millionaire—or even a billionaire! And as such he was right out of her league, even as a friend. Men like Jackson weren't friends. If they were anything at all, then they were trouble.

**Marion Lennox** was born on an Australian dairy farm. She moved on—mostly because the cows weren't interested in her stories!

In her nonwriting life Marion cares (haphazardly) for her husband, teenagers, dogs, cats, chickens and anyone else who lines up at her dinner table. She fights her rampant garden (she's losing) and her house dust (she's lost). She also travels, which she finds seriously addictive.

As a teenager Marion was told she'd never get anywhere reading romance. Now romance is the basis of her stories. Her stories allow her to travel, and if ever there was an advertisement for following your dream, she'd be it!

## Books by Marion Lennox

HARLEQUIN ROMANCE®
3694—ADOPTED: TWINS!*
3702—THE DOCTORS' BABY*
3726—A ROYAL PROPOSITION

*Parents Wanted!

# A MILLIONAIRE
# FOR MOLLY

*Marion Lennox*

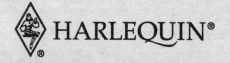

TORONTO • NEW YORK • LONDON
AMSTERDAM • PARIS • SYDNEY • HAMBURG
STOCKHOLM • ATHENS • TOKYO • MILAN • MADRID
PRAGUE • WARSAW • BUDAPEST • AUCKLAND

ISBN 0-373-03742-2

A MILLIONAIRE FOR MOLLY

First North American Publication 2003.

# CHAPTER ONE

OF ALL the times for Lionel to escape...

The reception area at Bayside Property was crowded and it was very, very noisy. Molly's cleaning team had declared an owner's wolfhounds were dangerous and they wouldn't go near her properties. Sophia, one of Molly's most valued landladies, was noisily furious that anyone could criticise her dogs. Jackson Baird was closeted with Molly's boss. And now...

'Lionel's gone,' Molly said in a voice that caused an instant hush. She was staring at her empty box in horror. 'Angela, did you...?'

And Angela had. 'I just showed Guy.' Molly's fellow realtor stared down at the empty box and her face reflected Molly's dismay. 'I swear that's all I did. Guy dropped in for coffee and he didn't believe you had a frog in your desk.'

'But you put the top back on, right?'

Angela caught her breath, thinking it through and becoming more appalled by the minute. 'I was just showing him when Jackson Baird walked in. Well, it *was* Jackson Baird!'

Enough said. Jackson Baird... The guy just had to enter the room and half the women present would forget their own names! What was it about the man?

Oh, sure, he was good-looking. He was tall, superbly fit and deeply tanned. And his face... You'd expect arrogance with Jackson's stature and reputation, but the man's face was almost Labrador-puppyish. It was a take-me-home-

and-love-me sort of face, with laughing grey eyes and a wonderful white smile.

Take-me-home-and-love-me? Molly read the society pages enough to know that women did just that. With inherited millions from Australia's copper mines, and a fierce business acumen of his own, the man had a reputation almost as vast as the number of zeros in his bank account.

So this morning he'd arrived and the whole office had stopped dead. Molly had just returned from inspecting Sophia's property, and even that voluble lady had been silenced as Jackson and his lawyer were ushered through.

'That's Jackson Baird,' Sophia had breathed as the entourage swept past into Trevor's inner sanctum. 'I've never seen him in the flesh. Is he a client of yours?' The elderly landlady had clearly been immensely impressed.

If he *was* a client it'd do the place an enormous amount of good, Molly had thought, and wondered which of their properties Jackson could possibly be interested in. They had some lovely bayside properties for sale, but surely none palatial enough to suit a man of his wealth.

'Jackson made me forget your frog,' Angela admitted. 'Well, you have to admit he's gorgeous.'

'Sure he's gorgeous,' Molly acknowledged, and then, more frantically, 'But where's my frog?'

'He must be here somewhere.' Angela dropped to her knees, her fair curls merging with Molly's dark ones as they met under the desk. They were both in their late twenties, and they were both extremely attractive, but there the resemblance ended. Angela treated the world as if it was there to give her a good time whereas Molly knew it would do no such thing. 'I mean, where can he have gone?'

Plenty of places. Trevor Farr's real estate agency was a small firm, and its owner, Molly's cousin, was a muddler.

The place was crammed with files almost to the ceiling. Somewhere among them was one green frog.

'Sam will kill me,' Molly wailed.

'We'll find him.'

'I should never have brought him to work.'

'You hardly had a choice,' Angela retorted.

No. She hadn't had a choice. Molly and Sam travelled on the same train—her eight-year-old nephew to Cove Park Elementary and Molly to Bayside Property. Their journey had almost been complete this morning before she'd realised why Sam's school bag was bulging, and she'd been horrified.

'You can't take Lionel to school.'

'I can.' Sam's bespectacled face creased into defiance. 'He misses me at home.'

'But the other kids...' Molly sighed. She knew only too well the social structure of the school. Hadn't she been in to see the headmaster only last week?

'Sam's being bullied,' she'd told him, and the man had spread his hands.

'We do our best,' he told her. 'Most kids in Sam's position would keep their heads down and stay out of trouble. But, even though Sam's about half the size of most third-graders, he matches it with the best of them. I'm afraid some of the children retaliate rather brutally. But of course you're right. The kid has pluck and we'll see what we can do.'

Which wasn't much, as Molly had thought when Sam had come home with yet another set of bruises. He laid himself open to pain, and if he took his frog to school there were kids there who'd delight in taking his pet from him. Who knew what would happen after that?

'It's too late to take him home now,' Sam told her, his

chin jutting forward in the Sam-against-the-world look she knew only too well.

It had been too late, so she'd brought Sam's frog to work.

Molly's job was very new. Her cousin had been reluctant to take her on in the first place, she'd had an appointment with Sophia at ten and was in no position to arrive late. So she'd arrived with Lionel's cardboard box under her arm and this was the result.

'Sam'll never forgive me.' Both girls were scrambling under the desk, oblivious to those above.

'Excuse me?' Sophia's tones from above the desk declared she was clearly not amused. 'Do I understand you're looking for a *frog*?'

'It's Sam's frog.' Molly's voice was almost a sob. She pushed her dark curls out of her face and started hauling the filing case from the wall. 'Help us.'

'I refuse to wait because of a frog. And as for helping...'

Angela reacted then. Molly was hauling furniture as if her life depended on it but Angela rose and put her hands on her hips. In the weeks Molly had worked for the agency she and Angela had become fast friends, and Angela would defend her friend to the death. 'Do you know who Sam is?' she demanded.

'Of course I don't, girl. Why should I?'

'Do you remember that awful accident about six months back?' Angela demanded. 'A truck came off the overpass and there were people in the car below. The adults were killed outright but there was a little boy trapped for hours.'

The woman's jaw dropped in horrified memory. 'Was that Sam?'

'Yes. And he's Molly's nephew.'

'Oh, no.'

'And now we've lost his frog.'

There was deathly silence. The three cleaners and Sophia

all let the enormity of this sink in, and then cleaners, land-lady, Molly and Angela—everybody started searching.

Unaware of the drama being played out in his outer office, Trevor Farr was growing more flustered by the minute.

At first he'd been delighted. He hadn't been able to be-lieve his luck. Hannah Copeland had telephoned this morn-ing and her call had stunned him.

'I've heard Jackson Baird is thinking of buying a prop-erty on the coast. There aren't many people I'd consider selling Birraginbil to, but Jackson may be one of them. My father used to deal with your grandfather, I believe—so you may contact Mr Baird on my behalf and if he's interested then I'll sell. That is, if you want the commission?'

If he wanted the commission? Birraginbil… Such a sale would set him up for life, Trevor had thought, dazed, and he'd made a phone call to Jackson's lawyer at once. He still hardly believed it, but now here was Jackson Baird in person, dressed for business in an Italian suit that screamed expensive, his eagle eyes cool and calculating, and waiting with polite patience for details.

The only trouble was, Trevor didn't yet have details.

So he did the best he could with what he had and tried to buy time. 'The property is on the coast, two hundred miles south of Sydney,' he told Jackson and his lawyer. 'It's Friday today. I'm otherwise engaged at the weekend, but would it be convenient if we drove down together on Monday?'

'I would have thought you'd at least have photographs.' Jackson's lawyer seemed deeply displeased. Like Trevor, Roger Francis had been caught on the hop, and the lawyer had reason to be unhappy. He'd had a property in the Blue Mountains lined up for Jackson's inspection, one where he'd pocket the sizeable commission himself and a bit more on the side. Unfortunately his secretary had taken the call about the Copeland place when he was out and the girl had taken it on herself to ring Jackson. Stupid woman! Now the lawyer was in a foul temper and Trevor's delaying tactics didn't help.

'Phone us when you have the details,' the lawyer snapped. 'If I'd known you had so little information we would never have come this far. You're wasting Mr Baird's valuable time.'

And then he paused. He stared down at the plush carpet in time to see a small green object. It jumped.

It was a small green tree frog—nature personified—and the lawyer knew exactly what to do with nature trying to edge its way into civilisation.

He lifted his foot.


'Do you think he could have jumped into Trevor's office when they opened the door?' Molly was staring in despair at the frogless back of the filing cabinet. 'Where else could he be?'

'I suppose he might have,' Angela said doubtfully, sitting back on her heels. 'I mean...everyone *was* staring at Jackson.'

Of course. Idiots. 'I'll look.' Molly rose.

'Trevor will kill you if you interrupt, Molly. He has *Jackson Baird* in his office.'

'I don't care if he has the Queen of Sheba in there. I'm going to look.' Molly put her nose against the glass pane in Trevor's door. And what she saw made her move faster than she'd ever moved in her life.

And Jackson?

One minute he was sitting between an irate lawyer and a confused realtor, trying to get some sense out of the pair of them. The next there was a flash of green against the

beige carpet, his lawyer's polished brogue raised to strike—
and a mop-headed, mini-skirted young woman launched
herself through the door and down at the carpet in what he
could only describe as a rugby tackle.

His lawyer's foot fell, but there was no longer a frog
underneath—instead there was a pair of hands, grasping
and cradling and protecting one small green frog as Roger's
foot stamped down.

'Ow!'

'Molly!'

'What the—?'

'Did you get him?'

'He stomped on him. He stomped on Sam's frog. Oh,
you brute!' Sophia Cincotta, breathing fire, was first into
the room after Molly, and she took one look at what was
happening and raised her handbag. She swiped at Roger
Francis. *'Murderer!'*

Angela came next, gazing down in horror. Molly was
lying full-length on the carpet, clutching Lionel as if her
life depended on it. 'Molly—your hand. Your hand's bleeding.'

'He's broken her fingers!' Sophia's handbag swiped
again, and the lawyer retreated fast to the other side of
Trevor's desk.

'Is Lionel okay?' Angela demanded.

'He's squashed,' Sophia retorted, bearing down on the
hapless lawyer. 'Of course he's not okay. Didn't you see
this brute step on him?'

'I thought those things were protected,' one of the cleaners volunteered.

'It'll be a toad, stupid,' someone else retorted. 'You're
supposed to kill them.'

'Not on my carpet.' Trevor's voice rose in bewilderment.
'Is this a frog? *A frog?* Molly, is this your doing?'

'Of course it's my doing,' Molly managed, peering between her bleeding fingers. 'And it's not a cane toad. Oh, heck, his leg looks… His leg looks broken.'

'Your fingers look broken,' Angela retorted, kneeling beside her and casting a murderous glance up at Roger Francis. 'It's him who's the toad.'

'Of all the unprofessional…' Roger was practically spluttering as he backed away from the handbag-wielding Sophia. 'Mr Baird, I suggest we look for a property elsewhere.'

Trevor collected himself at that, and moved between Molly and Jackson. He could see thousands of dollars worth of commission going up in smoke here. 'Mr Baird, I can't tell you how sorry I am. This is normally the most efficient of offices.' He glared down at Molly. 'My father persuaded me to employ my cousin because he felt sorry for her. But if she's going to offend major clients…' He tried for bluster, a weak man attempting importance. 'Molly, get up. You can collect your severance pay and leave.'

But Molly wasn't listening. She was still staring between her fingers. Lionel's leg was indeed hanging at an odd angle. It must be broken. She thought of the impossibility of mending broken legs on frogs.

What on earth was she going to tell Sam?

'Molly, get out.' This time Trevor's desperation broke through.

'You mean my frog's going to die and now I've been given the sack?' she managed, her voice a distressed whisper. Oh, great. How would they manage now?

'If you're going to upset Mr Baird—'

'She deserves to be sacked,' the lawyer hissed from the other side of the desk, and Sophia's handbag was raised again.

'Just a moment.' Jackson Baird rose and raised one hand. His voice was a soft and lazy drawl, but it had the capacity to halt everyone in their tracks. It was a voice of one born to command. He rose from where he'd been sitting and knelt by Molly, gently moving Angela out of the way. Immaculately dressed in his superbly fitted business suit, his night-black hair just casual enough for effect, his presence took over the room.

'What is he—a tree frog?' he asked Molly gently, and Molly wiped angry tears away with the back of her free hand. She sniffed and nodded.

'Yes.'

'And Mr Francis, here—my lawyer—has injured it?'

'I don't like insects,' Roger muttered.

'He's not an insect—' Molly started, but Jackson was still in control. Once again his voice cut through. 'It does seem hard that Miss Farr should injure her hand, see her pet hurt and lose her job all on the one day.'

Carefully he opened Molly's hand and took the frog into his own. Then he stood, solidly big, immaculately groomed—with a tiny green tree frog cradled in his palm.

A swipe of black hair flicked over his eyes and he brushed it back. The man needed a haircut—or maybe he didn't. There weren't many women who'd complain about how Jackson Baird looked.

And he looked amazing now. The tiny green frog, gazing upward with frog-like incomprehension, accentuated the sheer size and raw strength of the man. And yet he was all gentleness as his fingers carefully examined the tiny creature.

Trevor stared down at the frog in disgust, his expression squeamish. Wildlife had never been his strong point. 'Of all the ridiculous… Give it to me, Mr Baird, and I'll find a brick.'

But Jackson was concentrating entirely on the frog. 'You know, it looks a simple break, and there doesn't appear to be any more damage. I think we can fix this.'

Molly took a deep breath. And then another. She sat up, pulled her skirt down over her tights until she was almost respectable, and gazed up at Jackson in disbelief. 'You're kidding.'

He looked down at her... And then looked again.

She really was extraordinary, Jackson thought, taking her in for the first time. She had pale, almost translucent skin, a mop of glossy dark curls that clung around her face, huge brown eyes...

Frog! Concentrate on the frog, Baird, he reminded himself.

'Really,' he told her. 'We can't put it in a cast—'

'That'd be something!' Ever the clown, Angela interrupted from behind. Now that Lionel looked as if he might live, Molly's fellow realtor was appreciating the humour of the situation. 'We could make him crutches like Tiny Tim carries in the *Muppet Christmas Carol.*'

'Shut up, Angela.' Molly glowered as she struggled to her feet, and she hardly noticed as Jackson's free hand came out to steady her. This was serious. 'You were saying, Mr Baird?'

'I'm sure he can be fixed.' Two heads were now bent over one tiny green tree frog, and had no thoughts of anything else.

'We need to splint it,' Jackson told her.

'Crutches!' Angela chortled. 'I won't be content with anything less.' Then her laughter died. 'Molly, you're dripping blood on the carpet.'

'It's nothing.' Molly shoved her fist into her skirt but Jackson's hand came out and grasped hers. He held it up.

The skin had split over the knuckles and it was sluggishly bleeding. His face darkened.

'Damn you, Roger.'

'I was stamping on the frog. I didn't expect the stupid girl to—'

'It needs attention.'

'It does not.' Molly snatched her hand away and shoved it behind her back before he could see it further. 'It's only grazed. If Lionel can really be fixed—'

'Lionel?'

'My frog,' she told him, and he nodded with all the gravity in the world.

'Of course. Lionel. I see. And, yes, he can really be fixed.'

Molly looked up at Jackson as if he might be trying to trick her. 'How do you know?'

'There was a dam on our property when I was a kid,' he told her, taking in the look of strain around her eyes and puzzling a little over it. 'I spent my holidays raising tadpoles.' And escaping his parents. 'Anything you need to know about frogs, ask me.'

'It can heal?'

'It can heal.'

She took a deep breath and some of the tension eased. 'Then I'll take him to the vet.'

'I can splint it here, if you'll let me. But I can't fix your hand.'

'I'll take her to the hospital to fix that,' Angela said, putting in her two bobs' worth again and moving to hug her friend. 'If you fix the frog, then I'll fix Molly.'

'Angela!' Trevor's voice was an angry whisper, but Angela directed him one of her very nicest smiles.

'Mr Baird likes Molly's frog,' she said demurely. 'And we'd hate to upset Mr Baird, now, wouldn't we?'

At the look on her cousin's face Molly almost choked. 'Oh, for heaven's sake…' She took a deep breath and moved out of the protective circle of Angela's arm. 'Thank you all very much, but I'll take my frog to the vet and my hand just needs a sticking plaster. That's all. So I can take care of everything myself. And it doesn't matter if I leave.' She looked at her cousin and sighed. The man really was an idiot. Maybe it would be better if she walked away. 'After all, I'm sacked anyway.'

'You can't be sacked,' Jackson growled, and once again there was the stillness that his voice seemed to engender. He turned to Trevor, his finger lazily stroking Lionel's green back as he spoke. His eyes fixed Molly's cousin, impaling him like an insect on a pin.

'I came here to find out about a property. The information I have is tantalising, but it's scarcely detailed. I need more. And I need to see it. You say you're busy over the weekend?'

Trevor was totally flummoxed. 'Yes, but—'

'I've an option on another property until Monday, so I'd like to come to a decision before then. And I leave the country on Tuesday. Seeing the place for the first time on Monday hardly leaves time for negotiation.'

Trevor thought this through and backtracked fast. Negotiation—a wonderful word. It meant the man was a serious buyer. 'Of course. I'll just have to reschedule—'

'I don't believe I'll bother you,' Jackson told him, his voice cool and direct. 'I don't need you to show me the place. One of your employees will do just as well—'

'You still have time for another tour of the Blue Mountain property,' his lawyer interrupted, and was shot a look of dislike for his pains.

'Thanks, but I'm more interested in the Copeland place. Now, seeing as Miss Farr has just suffered an injury and a shock, what better way to help her recover than to take her away for the weekend? Mr Farr, I assume you weren't serious about sacking an employee for something so minor as bringing a frog to work?'

'No...' Trevor thought it through, and for Trevor thinking was a chore. 'Yes. But—'

But Jackson was no longer listening. 'Miss Farr, I would very much appreciate it if you could escort me to the property. Mr Farr, if your employee was to make such a sale I feel sure you'd be in a position to offer her her job back.'

Trevor gasped, but he wasn't completely stupid. Once again he could see a fortune in commission flying out of the window, and he grabbed at it with both hands.

'Maybe not. But I've just remembered I can come after all.'

'I don't wish to bother you.' Jackson's eyes were chilling. He turned to his lawyer. 'Or Mr Francis, for that matter. If the Copeland place is the farm I'm thinking of, then frogs are the least of the temptations for Mr Francis's ruthless shoe. So I believe Miss Farr and I will dispense with the middle men. Miss Farr, can you escort me to the Copeland property at the weekend?'

Molly took a deep breath. She stared wildly around—at Trevor—at the lawyer—and then at the tiny green frog sitting pathetically in Jackson Baird's big hand.

Jackson's eyes were gentle—kind, even—and she had no choice. Obnoxious cousin or not, she needed this job, and Jackson was offering her a way to keep it.

'It'll be my pleasure,' she told him. And she couldn't believe that she'd done it.

There was no disputing who was in charge. Ineffectual at the best of times, Trevor was completely overruled. Jackson was in organisational mode, and he hadn't been declared Australia's Businessman of the Year for nothing. The man exuded power.

'I'll meet you at Mascot Airport tomorrow at nine,' he told her, and she blinked.

'Um…we're flying?'

'I'll charter a helicopter.'

Oh, of course.

'You'll have a Section Thirty-Two prepared?'

A Section Thirty-Two… It would be a miracle if their lawyer could finalise the title and bill of sale by tonight, Molly thought, but Jackson Baird was expecting expertise to match his. 'Of course,' she told him.

'The house is set up so we can stay?'

'I believe there's a skeleton staff.' Trevor was fighting to stay in charge of a situation he had no control over. 'Mrs Copeland did say they'd welcome you, but I—'

Jackson wasn't in the mood for buts. 'Then that's fine.'

'I'm not happy about Molly going,' Trevor blurted out, and Jackson raised a mobile eyebrow.

'Isn't she competent?'

'She's extremely competent,' Angela shot at him, and received a look of approval from the millionaire for her pains.

'Maybe you're worried about the propriety of the situation?' Jackson's smile eased all before him. 'I should have thought of that. Miss Farr, if you're concerned about the propriety of escorting me to an unknown farm for the weekend I suggest you bring a chaperon. But no middle men. No cousin. An aunt, perhaps? Especially if she's another frog-lover?'

He was laughing at her, Molly thought, but she was too stunned to react. A chaperon. Where on earth would she find one of those overnight?

But Jackson had moved on. 'That's all, then. Mascot

airport, nine tomorrow, with or without a chaperon.' His eyes glinted suddenly with wicked laughter. 'Is that enough to take your mind off your sore hand and your frog?'

He thought it was, Molly thought numbly. He thought he just had to say jump and she'd put everything else aside and purr with pleasurable anticipation. And maybe normally she would. But there was still Lionel. Sam had trusted her with his frog. How was she going to tell him what had happened?

'Fine,' she said tonelessly, and his brows furrowed.

'You're still worried about your frog?'

'Of course.'

'You know, frogs do die.'

Damn the man, he was still laughing. 'You said you can fix him.'

'I did. And I can.' He turned to Angela. 'Will you take your friend to have her hand attended to now?'

But Molly wasn't moving. 'After Lionel is fixed.'

'You know…' His eyes were still puzzled. 'I hate to seem callous, but he is just a frog.'

'Just fix him,' she said wearily. Her hand was starting to throb and the shock of the last half-hour had taken its toll. Sure, Lionel was just a frog, but to Sam he was everything. Lionel had produced the first flicker of an outside interest she'd seen in the child since his parents' death, and that was so important.

'Just fix him,' she said again, and Jackson's dark eyes probed hers with something akin to confusion. What he saw in her face didn't help at all.

But he had a job to do.

'Okay, Miss Farr, I'll concede that your frog is important.' He put out a hand and touched her cheek. A fleeting gesture of reassurance. Nothing more. 'But so are you. If you won't go and get your hand seen to straight away then I'll do it for you. And then I'll fix your frog.'

'My frog first.'

'Your *hand* first,' he said in a voice that brooked no argument. 'Lionel's not dripping blood on the carpet. So sit and be cared for. Now!'

It was the strangest sensation.

Sit and be cared for... How long had it been since she'd done just that? Since her sister's accident the caring had all been on her side, and the sensation of cares being lifted from her shoulders was almost overwhelming.

'It's not deep.' Ignoring her protests, he was probing the abrasion on her knuckles, approving what he saw. 'I'm sure it doesn't need stitches.' He'd sent Angela down to the nearby dispensary and she'd come back with his requirements—lint, antiseptic, bandages and a soft reed—then stayed on to watch.

As did the rest of their audience. The cleaners had departed, as had Sophia Cincotta, but Trevor and Jackson's lawyer were going nowhere. Both of them, for different reasons, were bristling with disapproval.

But Molly was oblivious. She sat while this big man with the gentle eyes and the even gentler fingers knelt before her and probed and cleaned and carefully dressed her hand. It was unnerving, to say the least. It was...

Heck, she didn't know what it was. This man had a reputation a mile long where women were concerned and she was starting to see how he'd acquired it. He just had to touch her and...

'There. Okay?' He looked up at her and smiled, and she felt her heart do a crazy shift beneath her ribcage. Oh, for heaven's sake!

'Yes. Thank you. Now—'

'Now your frog.' He was still smiling at her, and it was a killer smile.

Angela handed over Lionel's box, where he'd been placed for safekeeping. She looked at her friend strangely as she did so. It wasn't like Molly to be this flustered. Interesting…

But Molly was still oblivious to anyone but Jackson. He had her mesmerised. He placed Lionel into her good hand and proceeded to do exactly what he'd promised, whittling a tiny splint, adjusting the leg so it was straight against the reed and then tying it carefully in place.

'It's as if he knows you're helping him,' Molly said, awed, and Jackson cast her another curious glance.

'Yes.'

'How long does he need to wear it?'

'Maybe a couple of weeks. You'll see the leg heal over.'

'I can't thank you enough.'

'My lawyer did the damage.' He lifted Lionel's box and seemed to approve of what he saw. Sam had lined the box with plastic and soggy plant litter for the frog's bed. 'This is a great little recuperation unit.' He lowered Lionel in and closed the box. 'All done.'

'Fantastic.'

'And now you. You've had a shock. Would you like Mr Francis and I to drop you home?'

But enough was enough. The man was starting to seriously unnerve her, and she had a business relationship to maintain.

'Thank you, but I'll be fine.'

'She'd like you to take her,' Angela volunteered, but got a glower from Molly. Molly took a deep breath and took hold of the situation. Somehow.

'I'll see you at nine tomorrow,' she told him.

He paused and looked down at her, still with that trace
of confusion in his eyes.

'With a chaperon?'

There was only one answer to that. 'Certainly with a
chaperon.'

He smiled at that, and once again his hand came out and
touched her cheek.

'Very wise. Okay, Miss Farr. I'll see you tomorrow at
nine. Take care of your hand. And your frog.'

And with that he was gone, leaving everyone in the office
staring after him.

'Molly, can I come? Please, can I come? You'll need help
and I can help you. I won't even cramp your style.' Jackson
was no sooner out of the door than Angela's clutch on her
arm intensified. 'I'd make a great chaperon.'

'Thanks, but I'll find my own chaperon.' Molly managed
a smile, albeit a weak one.

'*I* need to go with you,' Trevor told her. 'This is *my* real
estate firm.'

It might be, but it didn't seem like it. The family firm
had been handed down to this, the third Trevor Farr, and
under his expert guidance it showed every sign of heading
for bankruptcy. Trevor's father had spoken to Molly at her
sister's funeral and persuaded her to give the place a try.

'If you need a job in the city then I'd be grateful if you
could join the family firm. Work under Trevor for a while
as you get used to the city. You can learn the city trade
from him—and he can certainly learn things from you.
You're the best.'

Until then she'd worked selling farms from her base on
the south coast. Selling city property was a very different
thing, she'd discovered, and her cousin was proving to be

a millstone around her neck. Weak and ineffectual, he'd resented her competence from the start.

'I can cope on my own,' she told him now. She gave him a sympathetic smile. 'I have a strong feeling that Mr Baird doesn't want you or Mr Francis involved, and if his preferences mean a sale... How much did you say Mrs Copeland has on the place?'

Trevor swallowed. 'Three million.'

Molly practically gaped. Three million. Whew.

'Don't mess it up.'

'I won't.'

'Do you have someone respectable to take as a chaperon?' Trevor might be a dope but he wasn't completely heartless. Or he knew he'd have his father to answer to if anything went wrong. 'The man's got a reputation a mile long. Angela's not suitable.'

'Angela's definitely not suitable,' she agreed, managing a twinkle at her friend.

'You have someone in mind?'

'I do.'

Trevor paused, baffled at her lack of communication. 'I suppose it's all right, then.'

'I suppose it is.'

'Your hand's not too sore to keep working? You'd better get moving if you want a Section Thirty-Two prepared.'

'I'll do it now.' She flexed her fingers and winced, but Trevor was the only other person here capable of sorting the paperwork for such a property, and help from Trevor was the last thing she'd get.

'Right,' she said. 'Let's get on with selling Mr Baird a farm.'

# -CHAPTER TWO

THANK heaven Lionel wasn't dead.

Sam was stoic, as Molly had known he would be. He'd been stoic for six months now. He'd taken every bit of dreadful news on the chin. Now his face was pinched, but blank, and when Molly tried to hug him he held back. As always.

'I shouldn't have kept him in the first place,' he said miserably.

No. But then there was a no pets rule in their highrise apartment, so Sam had had nothing. They'd found the frog while they'd been crossing a busy Sydney street. It had been raining, there had been traffic everywhere, and Lionel had been sitting right in the middle of the road. He was a suicidal frog if ever there was one, and when Sam had pocketed him Molly hadn't protested. Where he'd been, the frog would have been doomed.

May he not be doomed now, she thought, looking at the intricate arrangement of ponds Sam had rigged up on the bathroom floor.

'I'll have to clean all this up when he dies.' The little boy put his hands in his pockets and tucked his chin into his chest. Molly knew there were tears waiting to get out. They'd wait a while. Molly cried. Sam didn't.

'He won't die. Mr Baird said so.'

'I guess frogs don't live very long anyway.'

Darn, it was so unfair. If Molly had her way, frogs would live for ever. But she had to be truthful. 'I guess they don't,' she agreed, and laid a hand tentatively on his arm.

But, as always, he pulled away. He was such an isolated child. It was as if losing his parents had made him afraid to trust.

And why should he trust? Molly thought bitterly. She couldn't even keep a frog safe.

'We've been asked to go to a farm for the weekend,' she said, trying to divert him. 'We'll take Lionel. It can be a convalescent farm.'

'A farm?'

'Yes.'

'I don't like farms.'

'Have you ever been to one?'

'No.'

'Then—'

'I don't like them. I want to stay here.'

Sure. And lie on his bed and stare at the ceiling as he did in every spare minute. 'Sam, Mr Baird has invited both of us.'

'He doesn't want me.'

'I'm very sure he does.'

'I don't want to go.'

'You're going,' Molly said with more determination than she felt. 'We're both going and we'll enjoy it very much.'

A weekend with Jackson Baird. Could she enjoy it?

There was a dangerous part of her mind that was telling her she could enjoy it very much indeed.


'Cara?'

'Jackson. How nice.' Cara might be on the other side of the Atlantic but her pleasure was tangible. 'To what do I owe the pleasure?'

'I think I might have found a property that could suit both our needs.'

'Really?'

'Really. It's been used as a horse stud in the past. It's in a magnificent location and it sounds wonderful. Do you want to get on a plane and come and see it?'

Silence. Then, 'Darling, I'm so busy.'

When was she not? Jackson grinned. 'You mean you'll leave it to me?'

'That's the one.'

'And if I buy it and you don't like it?'

'Then you'll just have to buy me another one.'

'Oh, right. Cara—?'

'Darling, I really can't come. There's something… Well, there's something happening that's taking all my attention, and I daren't say anything about it yet in case it evaporates in the mist. But I trust you.'

He grinned again. Another scheme. His half-sister always had schemes, but he trusted her implicitly, as he knew she trusted him. 'Millions wouldn't,' he told her.

'But you're one in a million. And don't you know it?'

'Yeah, and I love you, too.'

A chuckle and the line went dead, leaving Jackson staring down at the receiver.

Was this really a good idea?

'Okay, I give up. You're not going to ask me, are you?'

'Sorry?' Her friend stood on the doorstep late that night and Molly blinked. Angela was wearing a slinky, shimmery dress, her beads reached her waist and her hair was done up in some kind of fantastic arrangement of peacock feathers. Now she spun around for inspection.

'I'm off to a Roaring Twenties party. Guy is turning thirty, poor lamb, so we're having a last gasp at celebrating the twenties for him. Do you like my outfit?'

'I love it.'

'You know you could come.'

'And you know I can't.'

It was impossible, Molly thought. Social life was impossible.

Until Sarah died Molly had been running her estate agency on the coast. She'd been one of the most successful realtors in the business, going from strength to strength. Her love life, too, had been exceedingly satisfactory. Michael was the local solicitor and everyone had said they made the perfect couple.

Their combined life plans hadn't included Sam, though. 'Put him in a boarding school,' Michael had decreed when Sarah died, but Molly hadn't. Nor had she torn Sam away from his home in inner Sydney, though she was now starting to question the wisdom of moving here.

The city property market was hard to break into. Her cousin was a toad. Sam's school was less than satisfactory, and she couldn't afford to change him to a better one. Sam was miserable, and she was so darned lonely herself!

But leaving Sam with babysitters wouldn't solve anything. He woke with nightmares and she had to be there. After all, she was all he had.

'Hey, cheer up,' Angela told her, watching her face. 'You're about to spend the weekend with Australia's most eligible bachelor.'

She was, but the crazy thing was that she didn't want to go.

Like Sam, Molly still felt like closing all doors. Since Sarah's death the world had become a dangerous place. The newspapers hurled bad news at her, television shows seemed dark and threatening—and if it was like this for her, how much more so for a small boy who'd lost everything?

'Is the frog okay?' Angela asked.

'He seems great.'

'Thanks to Jackson.'

'If it wasn't for Jackson, Lionel wouldn't be injured.'

But Angela was determined to state his case. 'It was Jackson's lawyer who did the damage. Jackson himself was kind.'

'The man's dangerous. He has a reputation to put Casanova to shame.'

'Lucky you.' Angela sighed theatrically. 'My Guy is boring.'

'Boring is safe.'

'Now, that...' Angela tottered into Molly's living room on ridiculously high heels and fell onto a settee '...is why I'm here. To stop you being boring. To get back to my original question: you're not going to ask me, are you?'

'To do what?'

'To be your chaperon.'

'No.'

'You intend to take Sam, right?'

'Right.'

Angela took a deep breath. 'Well, I've decided to forgive you for not taking me. Though why I should, I don't know. Because with me there you wouldn't get a look-in. I'd sweep the man off his feet in two seconds flat.'

'But you have Guy. Your fiancé, remember?'

Angela grinned. 'That's right. I have Guy, and as nobility is my middle name—'

'Oh, please!'

'Don't interrupt me when I'm being noble. I've decided to offer my services as babysitter. For Sam. And for Lionel. There.' She beamed. 'How noble's that?'

'Very noble.' Molly winced. Her hand hurt, she was dead tired and she had mountains of paperwork to plough through before bedtime. And what her friend was suggesting was impossible. 'Angela, thanks for the offer, but you know I can't leave Sam.'

'He'll be fine with me.'

'He'll be stoic. He's always stoic and it breaks my heart.'

Angela's face softened. 'So share the care. I love the kid too, you know.'

'I know you do.' Angela's heart was huge. 'But, Angie, there's only a chink of room for loving anyone left in him, and that chink's for me. And that's only because I look like his mother.'

'And where does that leave you?'

'Right here. With him. Where I want to be.'

'So what are you doing now?'

'I'm going to bed.' It was a lie. She needed to ring Hannah Copeland for the property details, read everything she could find on the place and sort out the Section Thirty-Two. But if she told Angela that she'd drop everything and help.

'It's only nine o'clock.'

'I'm injured.'

'Not very injured. Come to our party.'

'And leave Sam? I don't have any choice in this, Angie, so let it be.'

Angela glared at her friend. 'It's so unfair.'

'Life's not fair.'

'It should be. You sure you won't change your mind about going alone? Leave Sam with me for just this once?'

'I'm sure.'

'Then I'll be here on Sunday night and I want a blow-by-blow description. Leaving out nothing.'

'You and Trevor both. He's already demanded a Sunday night debriefing.'

'He would.' Angela hesitated. You know...' Her face

changed and Molly knew what she was about to say. It would achieve nothing.

'Angela, don't.'

'Don't what?'

'Try to solve the problems of the world.' Molly gave her friend a push towards the door. 'Go on. Back to Guy.'

'Well, at least tell me what you're wearing tomorrow,' Angela demanded as she was propelled into the foyer.

'Boring. Business. Black suit. White shirt.'

That stopped Angela in her tracks. 'You're never wearing boring for Jackson Baird?'

'No. I'm wearing boring for me.'

'This is the opportunity of a lifetime.'

'To get myself seduced? I don't think so.'

'Molly, there's seduced and there's *seduced*. Boy, if Jackson Baird wanted to put his boots under my bed...' Angela chuckled. 'And honestly, Moll...' She turned and faced her friend. 'When I saw you both looking down at that little frog...'

Molly grinned at the picture that conjured up. 'Romantic, wasn't it?'

'It was,' Angela said firmly. 'You looked like you could be the future Mrs Jackson Baird.'

'Oh, yeah. In your dreams.'

'Well, why not? He's single. You're single. He's rich. That's a recipe for marital bliss if ever I heard one.'

'Angie, go!'

'Only if you promise you won't wear your business suit.'

'Maybe I should wear jeans.'

'No!'

'What would you suggest?'

'Something short. And slinky.' She chuckled again and looked down at her very slinky dress, complete with slit almost to her thigh. 'Something like this.'

'Sure. Complete with ostrich feathers. To show a man over a farm and to care for an eight-year-old.'

'And to marry a millionaire,' Angela added. 'Or a billionaire. Think big, girl.'

'I'm thinking goodnight,' her friend managed, and pushed her out through the door before she could say another word.

Jackson wasn't sure who he'd expected as Molly's chaperon. In fact if he'd thought about it at all—which he hadn't—he would have said that he didn't expect her to bring anyone—but the bespectacled child at her side was a shock.

As was Molly.

She looked stunning, he thought, watching her approach over the tarmac. There was no other word to describe her. She was about five feet four and neatly packaged, with a handspan waist and a halo of dark curls that bounced about her shoulders.

Yesterday she'd worn a business suit. Today she was wearing jeans and a soft white shirt that buttoned to the throat. It should have made her look prim, but instead it just made her look inviting. She looked fresh as a daisy, and as she got within speaking distance and smiled up at him it took a whole five seconds before he could answer.

'Good morning.' She was still smiling, but somehow he forced himself to ignore her lovely smile and tackle the issue at hand. Which was speaking. It should be easy, but it wasn't.

'Good morning,' he managed.

Unknown to Jackson, Molly was doing her own double take. Yesterday in his dark business suit Jackson had seemed very much an urbane man of the world—handsome, but completely out of her league. Dressed today in soft moleskin pants and a short-sleeved shirt, his throat and arms bare, he looked...

Well, he might be having trouble keeping to the business at hand, but so was she!

At least she could concentrate on Sam. 'Mr Baird, this is my nephew, Sam. Sam, this is Mr Baird.'

So she wasn't a single mum, Jackson thought. But if not why bring a child? It wasn't the sort of thing any woman he'd ever dated had done before. But then this was business, he reminded himself. Business! Not a date.

'Sam's brought Lionel along with us.' Molly motioned to the box under Sam's arm. 'We hope you don't mind, but we thought a convalescent farm was just what Lionel needed.'

'Right.' The frog. He took a grip, and held out a hand to Sam. They were standing on the helicopter pad and any minute now the machine would roar into life, drowning out all conversation until they wore headsets. 'I'm pleased to meet you, Sam.'

Sam looked gravely up at him as they shook hands, his eyes huge behind his glasses. 'Are you the man who trod on my frog?'

'I told you he wasn't,' Molly said gently. 'Mr Baird is the man who bandaged Lionel.'

'Molly says he might die anyway.'

'I didn't say that.' Molly sighed. 'I just said frogs don't live very long.' She cast a despairing glance at Jackson.

'I expect he will die,' Sam said sadly, clasping his box as if there were only a few short frogbeats left to his beloved Lionel. 'Everything dies.'

Jackson's gaze flew to Molly's, and Molly gave an inward shrug. There was nothing like getting to the hub of things fast.

'Sam's parents were killed in a car accident six months

ago,' she told him. If she'd had her way she would have warned Jackson, but it was impossible now. Her eyes didn't leave his, searching for the right response. 'Since then he's had a pessimistic outlook on life.'

Jackson nodded gravely, and to her relief his response was curt and to the point. 'I can understand that. I'm sorry about your family, Sam.'

Move on, Molly's eyes warned him, and she led the way. 'I told Sam that Lionel might live for ages yet.'

'I had a pet frog when I was eight,' Jackson said thoughtfully, rising to the occasion with aplomb. 'He lived for two years and then he escaped to find a lady frog. Maybe Lionel will do the same.'

Sam stared at him, disbelief patent. Silence. Let the helicopter start, Molly thought. This silence was desperate. But Jackson and Sam were eyeing each other like two opponents circling in a boxing ring.

Then Jackson seemed to come to a decision. His fast brain had worked overtime and now he stooped so his eyes were at Sam's level. Man to man.

'Sam, I'll tell you something else you might like to know.' His gaze met the little boy's and held. Molly was totally excluded. He was focused only on Sam. 'When I was ten years old my mother died,' he told him. 'I thought the end of the world had come, and, like you, I expected everything else to die. I expected it and expected it. It made me desperately frightened. But you know what? No one else died until I was twenty-eight years old. Ancient, in fact.'

Silence while Sam thought this through. Then he said, 'Twenty-eight's the same age as Molly.'

Jackson's deep eyes flashed up to Molly and there was the trace of laughter behind his serious gaze. 'There you go, then. I told you. Ancient. My grandpa died when I was twenty-eight, but for the time between being ten and being twenty-eight not a sausage died. Not even a frog.'

'Really?'

'Really.' He grinned. 'So maybe you'll be that lucky.'

'Maybe I won't.'

'But maybe you will.'

Sam considered. 'I've only got Molly left. And Lionel.'

'They both look healthy to me.'

'Yeah…'

'You're keeping them well fed? Lionel looks good and plump to me, and so does Molly.'

'Hey!' That was Molly, but she was far from minding.

For the first time Sam let himself relax. The corners of his mouth twitched into a quickly suppressed smile. 'That's silly.'

'Good feeding is important,' Jackson told him seriously. 'You can never overlook it. That and plenty of exercise. I hope you don't let Molly watch too much TV.'

Sam was grinning now, and the tension had disappeared like magic. 'She watches yucky programmes. With love and stuff.'

'Very unhealthy. I'd put a stop to that at once.' Jackson grinned with the wide, white smile that made Molly know exactly why the women of the world fell in love with him. Oh, for heaven's sake, the way he was treating Sam she was halfway to falling in love with him herself! She felt like hugging the man! He rose and held out his hand again to Sam. 'You want to come in my helicopter?'

Sam considered, and the whole world seemed to hold its breath. Then, as if coming to a major decision, Sam put out his hand and placed it in Jackson's.

'Yes, please,' he said.

Molly smiled and smiled, and Jackson looked at her

smile and thought suddenly, It's going to be a great weekend.

He hadn't expected efficiency. From the time he'd walked into Trevor Farr's office, Jackson had suspected if he wanted to find anything about Hannah Copeland's property he'd have to do it himself. But Molly's preparation stunned him. As soon as they were in the air she handed over titles, building plans, profit and loss statements, staff lists...

'How did you do this?'

'We do the same for all our clients.'

'Now, why don't I believe that?'

She threw him a wry grin. In truth this was the sort of property deal she loved—a farm with broad acres. She'd had to work until three this morning, but the presentation he had was first rate. Just like old times.

'Stop casting aspersions and read,' she ordered, so he did. But more and more he was aware of Molly and Sam in the seat opposite. Woman and child against the world...that was how they seemed, and their presence touched him as he hadn't been touched in a long time.

They?

*She* was a business acquaintance, he told himself, and Sam was nothing to do with him at all.

The Copeland place was stunning. The pilot took them on a wide sweep of the property. The farm started where the mainland formed a narrow strip and then broadened out to a vast spit reaching into the sea.

'The whole spit's the Copeland place,' Molly told him through the headsets, and he smiled and held up her printed plans. He already knew.

But no plans or photographs could do justice to this place. The sea lapped around the spit in sparkling sapphire glory. The beach was a wide ribbon of golden sand, and the hills and plains, dotted with placidly grazing cattle, looked lush and wonderful.

From the helicopter they saw streams trickling through hilly bushland towards the sea. There were waterfalls and tiny islands. As they came in to land a mob of kangaroos bolted for cover, and Jackson thought—This is paradise!

Paradise or not, he had to be businesslike, he told himself. This was a future for him and for Cara. He didn't make decisions with his heart. He made them with his head.

'It looks…well kept,' he said, and his words sounded lame even to him. He looked back to find Molly and Sam both gazing at him in surprise.

'Didn't you see the waterfall?' Sam demanded. 'It looks ace. Don't you think it looks ace?'

'Ace,' he agreed, and Molly grinned.

'I won't have to be a saleswoman if Sam's here.' She gazed out as the helicopter blades whirled to a halt. 'In fact, I don't think I have to be a saleswoman at all. If you have the money then this place will sell itself.' Her eyes danced, teasing. 'And if you don't have the money I can arrange a very appealing finance package.'

'I'm sure you can.' He said it dryly, but he was impressed for all that. She'd done her homework.

'There's no other property like this on the market anywhere else in Australia,' she told him. 'I don't know what you want this place for…' She let the question hang, but she wasn't enlightened so she let it slide. 'But whatever it is I think you'll find Birraginbil will provide it.'

'Birraginbil?'

'You know that Birraginbil is the name of the property?' She grinned. 'Now, ask me why I haven't put that in big letters at the top of your presentation.'

He looked at her, considering. She looked supremely

self-assured, he thought and it hit him suddenly that she was doing something she loved. Despite the appalling Trevor, the woman before him was an astute professional.

He grinned back at her, joining the game. 'So tell me what it means.'

'Place of leeches.' She chuckled at the look on his face, and the matching look on Sam's. 'Don't tell me you're scared of a few itty-bitty leeches!' She foraged in her handbag. 'Look.' She held out a small canister. '"Be prepared" is what they taught us in property sales school. Salt. If there's leeches here I'm ready for them.'

'Wow!' He was growing more and more impressed. She was some saleswoman!

'Are there really leeches?' Sam's voice was tremulous and Molly hugged him close.

'Yes, but only in the low-lying swamp. The estuaries around the beach are clear, and the deeper dams by the homestead are great for swimming.'

'And for frogs?' Jackson asked, and Molly raised her eyebrows. She smiled, grateful for his bringing Sam into the equation.

'I'll bet for frogs.'

'Can we show Lionel?' Sam was immediately interested.

'Yep.' She turned away from Jackson and he was aware of a sense of… He wasn't sure. Pique? Jealousy? Surely not. He thought he'd brought the frog into the conversation to make Sam smile, but now knew that he'd done it so Molly would smile. It was a strange way of getting a woman's attention—but women's attention was something Jackson didn't usually have to work at.

And now Molly had turned away. Molly was only giving him the business side of her while the personal side was directed purely at Sam. Which was fair enough. Sam needed her and Jackson didn't.

So why the sense of pique?

'We'll ask the farm manager to take Mr Baird on a sight-seeing tour. While he does that we'll find out where the frogs live,' she told Sam, and the irrational sensations Jackson was feeling only deepened. He tried to make it rational. After all, Molly *was* a realtor; surely it was *her* job to show the client around...

He'd work on it, he decided. And suddenly it seemed almost as important as seeing the farm. Seeing the farm with Molly...

## CHAPTER THREE

THE arrangement was that the helicopter would collect them the following day, and no sooner had it lifted from the pad and roared off into the sun than an elderly couple appeared. At the sight of Jackson, Molly and Sam, their faces almost split with delight.

'A family,' the elderly lady breathed, and she gripped her partner's hand. 'See, Gregor, what did I tell you? A family!'

'We're not a family.' Molly spoke swiftly and Jackson felt an irrational pang of disappointment. Misconception or not, it had felt good—for a moment. Which *was* irrational. Wasn't it?

But of course Molly was right. If he was seriously interested in this property then he had to get off on the right foot from the start.

'Miss Farr's acting as realtor for Miss Copeland,' he told them. 'I'm Jackson Baird, the potential buyer.' He smiled at Sam, half hidden behind Molly. 'And this is Sam, Molly's nephew. He and his pet frog, Lionel, have come along for the ride.'

The elderly woman took a deep breath and made a recovery. 'Then, family or not, we're very pleased to meet you,' she told them. 'I'm Doreen Gray, Miss Copeland's housekeeper, and this is my husband, Gregor. Come on in. I'll make us a cup of tea and we can get to know each other.'

And that set the tone for the weekend. Doreen and Gregor had no concept of formality. Jackson, Molly and Sam were treated as very special guests. Indeed, they might have been family for the welcome they received.

'You don't see many people?' Molly ventured over her third scone, and she knew straight away that she'd hit the nail on the head.

'No, dear, we don't,' Doreen told her. 'Time was when the Copelands used to have every important family in Australia staying here. We have nineteen bedrooms, would you believe? And we filled them all. But Mr and Mrs Copeland passed away almost thirty years back and Miss Copeland never was one for socialising. She moved to Sydney ten years ago and the place has been almost abandoned.'

'Is it run down?' Jackson's brows creased, but Doreen's face stiffened and she offered him another scone as if to say—Does this look like the product of a farm let go?

'It most certainly isn't. Miss Copeland would never stand for that. We run over three thousand head of cattle. At mustering we have over a dozen men. And once a month I have a girl in from town to do the house from stem to stern. If you wanted to fill those bedrooms tomorrow you'd find nothing amiss.'

'I'm sure I wouldn't.' Jackson looked appreciatively about him. The kitchen was just as farm kitchens ought to be—big and warm and welcoming, with a vast firestove that stretched almost from wall to wall. It gleamed with cleanliness—no mean feat, he guessed, when the house was well over a century old.

Cara would like this kitchen.

No, she wouldn't. He gave a rueful inward grimace. What was he thinking of? Cara wouldn't step foot in a kitchen unless she was dragged.

But she'd love the rest of the place. The house was fabulous. Vast bluestone walls were ringed by a wide veranda that ran the full perimeter of the house. Every room seemed to have French windows. The curtains wafting outwards in the breeze looked fresh and new, and the whole place had instant appeal.

He looked across the table and found Molly's eyes on him, assessing, and he guessed she was right in business mode.

'It's great, isn't it? You know, you're the first person we've shown it to.'

'I know that.'

'You won't be the last.' She turned to Mrs Gray and smiled. 'I hope you bake scones every time I bring prospective buyers down here. These are delicious.'

It was a tactful way of saying Jackson was first in a queue and there were others who'd be interested if he wasn't. He smiled, acknowledging she had a point but refusing to be hurried. 'But I have first option, right?'

'I believe you have first option until Monday.'

'Very generous.'

'We aim to please.' She smiled across the table at him, and he found himself staring. She was charming. Intelligent. Organised. Beautiful...

He found himself looking down at the ring finger on her bandaged left hand—just in case—and felt a ridiculous twinge of pleasure when he discovered it was bare. And then he had to jolt himself back to hear what she was saying.

'Mr Jackson would like to see over the farm,' she told Gregor. 'Can you show him around?'

'Oh, my dear...' The elderly farmer's face fell.

'Is there a problem?'

'I can't do it,' Gregor said heavily. 'My legs won't take me.'

'I didn't mean walk,' Molly told him. 'I assume there's a vehicle?'

'The Jeep's in for a service. If we'd known you were coming… But Miss Copeland only rang last night to tell us you were on your way.'

'There's the farm bike,' Doreen said. 'But it only holds one. Then there's the horses, but Gregor's hip can't take it.'

It nearly killed them, Molly saw, to admit that they were getting old and needed help. Gregor's face was anguished.

'I can go by myself,' Jackson said gently, reacting to the old man's distress. 'Miss Farr…' He cast Molly a sideways look and decided on informality. '*Molly's* given me excellent maps, and if you have a horse then I can ride.'

'But you could fall off.' Doreen was practically wringing her hands. 'There's rabbit holes and heaven knows what else. You'll want to see everything, and the only way to see it properly is by horse, but…'

'You can't go alone,' her husband added. He turned to Molly and she could see what an effort it cost him to ask. 'Unless you ride, miss?'

'I ride,' she said briefly, and received another look of astonishment from Jackson. One surprise after another… City realtors, it seemed, were not expected to ride.

She hesitated. Sam was right beside her, pressing close. His insecurity was almost tangible. 'But Sam can't.'

'We'll look after Sam.' Doreen beamed at this easy solution to the problem. 'It would be our pleasure.' Then she addressed Sam, adult to adult. 'I'm making a pavlova for supper,' she told him. 'Have you ever made one?'

Sam hesitated. 'No, I…'

'Would you like to learn? I need help to pick the strawberries for the top.'

'And we're hand-rearing a calf,' Gregor added, seeing

where Doreen was headed and putting in his two bobs' worth. 'She needs bottle-feeding. Seems to me you're just the sort of lad who'd be able to do that.'

'And did you say you have a frog in that box?' Doreen asked. 'After we've done our jobs, Gregor and I will walk you to where there are a thousand frogs. And tadpoles to match.'

It was too much. Sam gave a shy nod and the tension in the room eased like magic.

Molly let her breath out in a rush. Darn, everywhere she looked there were conflicting demands, but these two lovely old people had given her time off. Wonderful...

'Can you really ride?' Jackson demanded. 'Or do you mean you can sit on a riding school hack?'

The toad! 'Try me,' she retorted, and turned to Gregor, excluding Jackson nicely. He deserved to be excluded. 'According to my livestock lists you have some fine horses.'

'They'll be frisky,' Gregor warned. 'They haven't been ridden since muster.'

'The friskier the better,' she told him. 'I can't wait.'

And the thing was settled.

'It'll take you the best part of the day to get around,' Doreen added. 'I'll put together a picnic for your saddle-bags. You have a lovely day for it.' She beamed. 'There. That's settled. You have a lovely ride and see the property and Sam will have fun with us. Isn't that lovely?'

What was her story?

Jackson watched as Molly helped catch and saddle the horses, and by the time they were mounted he knew she hadn't spoken lightly when she'd said she could ride. She looked as if she'd been born in the saddle. Her roan mare was skittish as be damned, but she held her as steadily as Jackson held his bay. Then, as Gregor let them go and the mare skittered sideways, she turned a laughing face towards him.

'They won't settle until they've had a gallop, and the home paddocks are safest. Race you to the far gate.' Before he knew what she was about she was off, the mare galloping like the wind and Molly riding her with an attitude that spoke of sheer joy at being alive.

Or more. Of release.

It was quite a sight. It took Jackson about ten valuable seconds before he recovered himself enough to turn his attention to his own horse—by which time she had an unassailable lead, and she'd paused and was waiting when he reached her at the far end of the paddock.

'What kept you?' she demanded.

'I thought businesswomen always let their clients win,' he complained, and received another of her lovely, throaty chuckles.

'Whoops. But I'm on a sure thing here. If the rest of this property is as good as this then it'll sell itself.'

She had a point. The more he saw the more he liked. But he wasn't just assessing the property!

'You're not a bad horseman,' she was saying, and it drew a grin.

'Gee, thanks,' he told her dryly. 'If I didn't just know that flattery was good for business...'

'Didn't I tell you this wasn't business? The property will sell itself, with no need for idle compliments to get a buyer in the mood.'

'So you did.' His mood was lightening by the minute. She was making him feel free of the restrictions he usually surrounded himself with.

Those restrictions were his by choice, he told himself. His life, his work. Cara. They were all his choice.

But it didn't hurt to take a break.

'Where did you learn to ride?' he asked as they turned their now amenable mounts towards the hills.

'On the back of a dairy cow.'

That had his eyebrows hiking upwards. 'You're kidding?'

'Nope. My parents ran a small country newsagency. I was jealous of all the kids who had farms, so when they saddled up their horses I made do with Strawberry. Strawberry was our house cow.'

His lips twitched. 'Don't tell me. You rode her to school?'

'Well, no. I couldn't ride her when Dad was looking. It put her off her milk.'

'I'd imagine it would.' He was feeling more and more dazed. A sudden vision of Molly on a dairy cow crossed his mind and he blinked it away. It had the power to unsettle him completely.

But she was unaware. 'This next bit's the murky bit,' she told him, motioning to a tract of swamp land. 'I'd guess this is where the leeches are. You want to stop and look closer? If so I'll go over to the next hill and wait.'

'What—scared of a few leeches?'

'Yes,' she said firmly. 'Despite my salt canister. But off you go. Tread where no man has trod before. After all, isn't that your reputation?'

'Is it?' he demanded, startled, and to his surprise she took him seriously, her gaze raking him from head to toe. Assessing. It was a strange kind of glance and it unnerved him.

'They say you're ruthless. In business you'll stop at nothing.' Her tone was uncommitted.

'You're a businesswoman yourself.' Her unspoken criticism rankled.

'So I am.'

'But you have limits?' His tone was probing.

'As I imagine you have.'

'Like leeches.'

'As you say.' She grinned, and the sudden unexplained tension eased a bit. 'Does that mean you're not hiking through the swamp like a true hero?'

'I can see everything I need to see from up here,' he said with what he hoped was dignity, and her chuckle unnerved him all over again.


The swamp was the worst of the whole place. The rest was sheer magic. They skirted the swamp and made their way to the sea. Here the paddocks butted the dunes and the lush pasture was cropped by sleek, well-fed cattle. They looked the most contented cattle Jackson had ever seen, and he thought, Well, why not? I'd be pretty happy if this was my lot.

They drifted down onto the sand without speaking. A kind of contented silence had built between them. Jackson headed his horse wherever the urge took him and Molly was content to follow. Down on the sand, he headed for the shallows and then, letting that same urge do as it willed, urged his horse into a gallop. Molly followed. They rode side by side, the waves splashing up over their feet and the salt spray misting their faces. When they finally drew to a halt Molly was flushed and laughing and bright with happiness.

'That was wonderful.'

'You never learned to do that on a cow.'

'I did get a horse,' she admitted. 'Eventually.'

'So what in heaven's name are you doing in the city?'

'I work in the city.'

'Your whole attitude screams farm girl.'

'Gee, thanks. I thought I'd hidden the hayseeds well.'

'We had a farm ourselves,' he told her. 'When I was a kid. My mother owned a holding north of Perth and I spent every moment I could there. And you don't spend years of your life on a farm without learning a city slicker from a…'

'From a hayseed?' Her eyes danced. Honestly, she was gorgeous. He had a sudden almost irresistible temptation to lean over, take her face in his hands and—

Whoa. Where was this headed?

Business. Back to business, Baird. Now!

'From a hayseed,' he agreed weakly, and her sudden thoughtful expression had him wondering. Was she feeling what he was feeling? How much a woman of the world was she? Would it hurt to…?

Hell. Business!

'We'd get a view of the whole place from the cliffs,' he managed, motioning sideways, and if she could tell his thoughts were disordered she didn't let on. 'And it'd be a great spot for lunch.'

'So it would,' she said equitably. 'Okay, MacDuff. Lead the way.'

But the tension didn't ease.

He didn't react like this to women, he thought as he finished off the last of Doreen's sandwiches. Molly had abandoned him on the picnic rug. She'd moved a little way away, aiming to give him space to admire the view. Which was spectacular. He should be concentrating on it entirely instead of being so darned conscious of her that he couldn't think straight.

Damn, he was never like this with women. He didn't have to be. There'd always been a woman by his side, ever since his first date aged about fifteen. His combination of money and looks and power proved a powerful magnet that few could resist. And after the last disaster…

Play it light, he told himself, and then he thought, Well, maybe a swift liaison wouldn't do any harm. Molly wasn't exactly a teenager. The laughter glinting in the back of her eyes told him she was very aware of his attributes and was sizing him up. She was no fool. She wouldn't get the wrong impression, as had…

Whoa!

'There's wine here,' he called to her, hauling his thoughts back to practicalities. She was a whole twenty feet away, perched on the branch of a low-growing gum. Below them were the cattle pastures and the slow-moving river drifting out to the sea. The sun was on her face and her eyes held a strange tranquil expression.

How to describe it? It was as if she was hungry, he thought. But not hungry for food. Hungry for life? It was as if she was soaking in every minute of this as if it'd have to last a lifetime.

'I don't need wine,' she told him, hardly changing expression. 'I don't need anything.'

Her expression intrigued him. 'Why do you work in the city?' he asked curiously. 'When it's obvious your love is here?'

'Sam's home is in the city.'

'You moved there when Sam's parents died?'

'Wouldn't you?'

The question took him aback. Would he? He didn't know, he thought. As the privileged child of wealthy parents he'd never been asked to make the sort of sacrifice Molly was making. Any kind of sacrifice, for that matter.

'Kids are adaptable,' he told her, thinking things through. 'I assume you were living in the country at the time of the accident. Couldn't Sam have moved there with you?'

'I tried,' she said briefly. 'It was a disaster.' Should she tell him the whole sad story of Michael? No way. She'd let herself love a rat and it had taken a tragedy to show that to her. She could no longer live in the same small town as Michael. It was hard enough to know he was in the same country.

'Sam's parents lived in a plush city apartment and he goes to an inner city school,' she told him. 'He needed continuity. So I moved.'

As simple as that. 'But aren't you—?'

'Did you note the carrying capacity of those pastures?' she demanded, switching track with a definite purpose. 'It's amazing. I've never read such figures for non-dairy country, and that's without putting added nutrients on the pastures—something that hasn't been done for years. If you were to invest in superphosphate—'

'I'll invest in superphosphate.'

Her eyes narrowed. 'You mean you'll buy?'

He corrected himself. '*If* I buy, I'll invest in superphosphate.'

'It's a great buy.'

Silence. Somewhere a kookaburra started up, its raucous chortle ringing through the bushland. From where they were settled they could hear the faint crashing of waves on the beach below, and the breeze was a gentle whisper through the gums overhead. The place was indeed magic...

'This place will sell in two minutes in the open market.'

'There's not a lot of buyers with the cash needed to buy a place like this.'

'I know at least five,' she said promptly. 'You want me to name them? You decide against this place and I'll be on the phone to them in minutes. They don't know it's on the market or they'd be beating a path to our door.'

He gave a rueful grin. 'You do a very pressured sales pitch.'

She smiled. 'That's my job.'

'Selling farms?'

Her smile died. 'Yes.'

'But you now sell city properties.' He was still probing, still searching for what lay beneath. 'Do you enjoy that?'

'Of course I do.'

'There's no "of course" about it. You're a country girl, born and bred. Even I can see that.'

'Well, how about you?' she asked, trying again to change direction. 'You spent a lot of your childhood on a farm. Why are you thinking of buying this place? Are you returning to your roots?'

'You could say that.'

'From all I hear you spend most of your time overseas.'

'Until now.'

'So you're thinking of settling down here.' The idea, she decided, appealed to her. This place and this man seemed to suit each other. He sat with his back against a rock, the sun on his face as he gazed out over the pastures to the sea beyond. He looked at peace. Like a man coming home. A man who belonged.

'Maybe,' he said at last.

Still she probed. 'Are you thinking of getting married?'

His face stilled. 'Why do you suggest that?'

'I don't know.' She shrugged. It was none of her business after all. 'I guess, when a man thinks of settling…'

'And Mrs Gray would like a family here?'

'There is that.' She smiled as the inexplicable note of tension eased. 'I hope you'd oblige. After all, it is extremely important to keep the hired help happy.'

'By having a family?' He assumed an expression of horror. 'No way. Not even for the Grays. Maybe I'll borrow Sam from time to time.'

She thought that through and approved. 'He'd like that.'

'So, despite you staying in the city, Sam's not happy?'

Drat, they were talking about her life again, and she shouldn't do it. He was a client. She knew better than to mix business with pleasure. They stayed absolutely apart.

But it was so tempting to talk of Sam. She was so worried about him, and Jackson was looking at her with calm grey eyes that said he was really interested. He really cared.

'No.' She sighed. 'He's not happy. I guess I can't expect that—his parents have only been dead six months. But...' Her voice trailed off and she bit her lip. He couldn't really care.

Only it seemed he did. 'How did he come by the bruises on his face?'

'He takes on the world.'

'Can you explain?'

Unwise or not, the temptation to unload her worries was irresistible. Jackson's shoulders were so broad—maybe it wouldn't hurt to burden him a little.

'He's so darned little,' she told him. 'He's the smallest kid in his class, but he won't take a back seat. He stands up for himself, no matter what. If a bigger kid pushes in front of him Sam will shove back, regardless of the consequences—and he always comes off second best. The school's not great, but I can't afford to move him.'

Jackson thought that through. 'There's money problems?'

'My sister and her husband didn't believe in insurance. And they lived life in the fast lane. There were debts.'

'I see.' And he did. More than she knew. He could guess by the set look of her chin just what sort of obligations she'd shouldered. 'He's some responsibility.'

'As you say.'

There was silence again, but this time it was different. There was no tension. It was almost as if they knew what the other was thinking.

He seemed…a friend, Molly thought inconsequentially. It seemed she was being offered friendship in an unlikely place—but it was friendship, regardless. She'd heard the note of caring in his voice and it made her blink back tears.

Drat the man. He had the capacity to get under her skin. And why? Because he was big and handsome and gentle and…

And a millionaire—even a billionaire! As such he was right out of her league, even as a friend. Men like Jackson weren't friends. If they were anything at all then they were trouble.

She bit her lip and stooped to pack their picnic things. 'It's time we were getting on. There's still plenty to see.'

'So there is.' But his gaze was on her face and his eyes were thoughtful.

'So, help me,' she demanded, letting a note of irritation enter her voice. 'It won't all fit in *my* saddlebag.'

'And you're not my servant?' His tone was faintly teasing and Molly flushed.

'No, Mr Baird, I'm not your servant,' she snapped, and kept on packing.

But still he didn't help. He stood looking down at her stooped figure, and there was a very odd expression playing beneath the thoughtfulness of his features.

She was some lady! The thought hit him out of nowhere, and he didn't have a clue what to do with it.

# CHAPTER FOUR

THEY rode for three hours and they hardly talked. There was no need.

The property did indeed sell itself, Molly decided as they moved from one paddock to another. Each seemed better than before. This was a tiny paradise cut off from the outside world. The more she saw, the more three million seemed very cheap.

But it wasn't for her to say. Hannah Copeland had named her price and it was up to Jackson to say yes or no. If he said no then she'd contact Hannah and advise her to increase her asking price the next time she showed anyone...

'What are you thinking?' Jackson demanded, and Molly discovered that he'd been watching her. Were her thoughts transparent? She hoped not.

'You're thinking of upping the price,' he said bluntly, and she had to smile.

'Um...yes.'

'You think three million is cheap?'

'It is, and you know it is.'

He gazed around him and had to agree. 'Yep.'

'So, if I ask you to pay more...?'

'I'd tell you to take a cold shower.'

'That's blunt.' She grinned. 'But you agree it's a bargain?'

'I'd imagine there are strings attached. Are there?'

'There may well be. If you're really interested I'll contact Miss Copeland this evening and ask what she has in mind.'

'It may well be taking on Doreen and Gregor.'

She thought that through and figured it was a distinct possibility. The elderly couple had been here for most of their lives and to move them on would be cruel. 'Would that be a problem?'

'Family retainers are the devil.'

'I'd imagine they'd be loyal.'

'They should be put out to pasture and you know it.'

She looked across at him, still considering. 'Would you be the one to put them out to pasture?' Suddenly his answer was absurdly important. She knew what his answer should be—his reputation was as a ruthless businessman, after all—but in the short time she'd known him she'd seen the kindness of the man, and it was desperately important that he still display it.

He was still watching her face, and it seemed the man could still read her thoughts.

'Just because I splinted a frog's leg, don't think I'm a soft touch.'

'You were nice to Sam as well.'

'Okay, I was nice to Sam,' he conceded. 'Neither of those things cost me money.'

'And if they had—would you still have done them?'

'It depends entirely on how much. Any more than tuppence-halfpenny and I'd have consulted my accountant.'

She gave a chuckle and turned her face to the sun. She hadn't felt this good for years, she thought. Or…since Sarah died. Jackson had given her this day, and for that she had to be grateful. 'You will keep Doreen and Gregor on your payroll?'

'I haven't agreed to buy the place yet.'

She gave him a cheeky grin. 'Neither you have.'

'And I mightn't.'

'Yeah, right.' She knew she had the man seriously hooked. Things were looking very good. Very good indeed. But she didn't press the point. Instead she headed her horse down towards the river. 'If we follow the river we'll end up home,' she told him.

'No.'

'No?'

'We'll end up swimming,' he told her. 'It looks fabulous.'

'It looks wet.'

'Chicken!'

'I didn't bring a costume,' she told him. 'And respectable realtors don't strip to their bras and panties and go swimming with clients. It's absolutely not done.'

'What a pity.'

'It is a pity.' Another grin. 'But don't let me stop you.'

'From stripping?'

'Be my guest. I promise I won't produce a camera. Or if I do it'll be a very small one.'

'You know, I wouldn't be the least bit surprised if you're carrying one, along with your leech repellent,' he said bitterly.

She laughed. Her lovely chuckle rang out, free and joyous, and he sat still in his saddle and stared at her. Then as she moved off he had to make an almost visible effort to follow.

What on earth was happening to him? He didn't have a clue!

But in the end she did swim. In the end she didn't have a choice. Molly reached the river before Jackson, and by the time he reached her she was staring across the slow-moving current, her laughter completely disappeared.

'What's wrong?' His gaze followed hers and found what she was looking at. 'Oh...'

Upriver, a couple of small logs had fallen over a cut in the bank, and twigs and leaf matter had piled high. They'd seen the debris as they'd ridden, and it didn't take a genius to figure out what had happened next.

A tiny kangaroo, barely half grown, had hopped out onto the debris, thinking it a firm foothold. It wasn't. The debris around the joey told its own story. The whole mat had given way and the baby kangaroo was now drifting helplessly towards the sea.

On the far bank a full-grown 'roo was following her offspring's progress in obvious terror. She was leaping along the bank and then gazing back to the bushland, knowing she shouldn't venture far from cover but compelled to follow her baby. Back in the shadows were the remaining mob, sleeping out the heat of the day and oblivious to the drama being played out nearby.

And it was drama. The joey would be out to sea in no time—or washed away and drowned. Jackson turned to Molly and found her off her horse and tugging at her boots.

'What the hell are you doing?'

'I can reach him.'

'You'll be swept out to sea.'

'Not me. I'm a country girl—remember? Born and bred by the sea. I can swim like a fish.'

He was down from his horse, grasping her arms to restrain her. 'Don't be stupid. It's only a 'roo.'

Only a 'roo... The words hung between them. She gave an angry wrench but he held her still.

'Molly, no.'

'I can do it. Only a 'roo? Yeah, like it was only a frog. I can't let it drown.'

'And how do you propose grabbing it? You'll be cut to pieces.' He looked at her face and saw implacability. With an inward groan he turned to assess the river.

Maybe she was right. Maybe the thing was possible. The water looked clear enough. Apart from the tumble of debris around the 'roo there seemed little enough to trap and hold, and the clear running water appeared sand-bottomed and friendly.

'I'll go in,' he told her.

'You can't!'

'Why not?' He was hauling the saddle from his horse. 'We'll need the saddlecloth to hold the joey. Help me.'

'You…' She took a deep breath and steadied, sanity prevailing. 'If you drown, Trevor will kill me. "Millionaire Killed by Baby Kangaroo." I don't think so.'

'I don't intend to drown.'

They glared at each other. 'So we'll go in together,' Molly snapped.

'Don't be ridiculous.' He had the blanket free now, and was concentrating on hauling off his boots.

'Who's ridiculous? One in, all in.' And Molly's shoes were kicked aside and she entered the water before he did.

Jackson didn't follow. Not straight away. He paused and waited.

It never paid to jump in at the deep end. Hadn't he learned that over and over in his business life? And what was needed here was a bit of calm-headed logic.

Molly seemed to know what she was doing, and, watching her, he was reassured. She'd dived in downstream and was fighting the current to reach midstream before the joey reached her. He watched for a whole three seconds—

enough to see her move with strokes that were strong and sure. Enough to see that she was safe.

Okay, then. Molly was fine. Now for one 'roo. He tied the saddlecloth around his hips, strode swiftly downstream and dived in after the pair of them.

Molly was a good swimmer, but Jackson was better. Where she cut diagonally through the current, Jackson simply stroked straight across.

The joey was still floating towards them, his two small ears and his huge eyes almost all they could see above the surface. The debris he was floating on was breaking apart and his platform was sinking by the minute.

Jackson reached midriver first, and trod water as he waited. Molly was slightly upstream, but coming fast.

As she reached him he held out a hand and grasped—strong, sure and determined. Molly had enough time to register the strength of his hold, and ten seconds later the joey cannoned into the wall they'd created with their linked arms.

The kangaroo might only be half grown, but with his underwater platform of branches he seemed to weigh a ton. And the little creature was terrified—as much of these two strange humans as he was of the river. He backed away. His platform wobbled, steadied, wobbled again.

Let him not jump…

Combined, Jackson and Molly formed a trap. They were linked by joined hands, and the joey was locked between them, their arms making a triangle with the 'roo's platform in the apex. But they were all being swept inexorably towards the river mouth.

And at the river mouth…rocks.

'Get back to shore,' Jackson gasped at Molly. 'You can't do this.'

'I can.'

'I'll do it. You go back.' He tried to disengage their hands to leave her free, but she was having none of it.

'No. Let's both try.'

'Molly, you don't have the right. Remember Sam.'

Great. Here she was, risking life and limb, and he was reminding her of her responsibilities. As if she needed reminding. She wasn't risking anything, she thought angrily. She could do this!

'We're wasting effort,' she gasped. 'Just swim.' Their hands stayed linked. His hold was sure and strong, and she wasn't relinquishing it for the world. The joey was between them, the little creature's eyes on a level with theirs. His terror was palpable.

And still he backed away. The 'roo wouldn't stay on the platform while they guided him ashore. He'd jump any minute.

'I'll get behind him,' Jackson gasped. 'Stay where you are.'

There was one branch larger than the rest that formed the joey's foothold. Molly grasped it lightly, trying not to pressure it any further underwater. She didn't want the joey washed off.

Then she tried to keep the joey's attention on her. 'Watch me,' she gasped, figuring what Jackson intended before she was told. She bobbed up and down and kept on talking as the joey backed a little more. She was trying to keep the joey's eyes fixed on her.

And then Jackson was behind him. He trod water for a moment, steadied, and raised the sodden blanket. Before the joey could react he dropped the rug, and in one swift movement he had the joey trussed like a Christmas parcel.

The razor-tipped paws slashed, but the cloth was made of thick felt. Jackson swore, steadied, swore again and floated on his back. The wrapped joey writhed furiously on his chest, but finally was still.

'I can't do anything with him here,' Jackson gasped. It was all he could do to hold on. 'Can you tow me?'

It was some question—but she could. Molly released the platform of twigs to let it rush on towards the sea, and then fought to get behind Jackson. She cupped her hands under his chin, lay back, then kicked out and started to tow. Jackson kicked in unison and slowly they moved towards the bank.

It took all their strength—more than all their strength— to move the joey towards the shore, and afterwards Jackson never could figure out how they had. He surely couldn't have done it on his own.

Molly's strength was amazing. He could kick, but nothing more, and that alone wasn't enough to battle the current. But somehow she found the strength to tow not just herself but him, and the kangaroo with him.

The river broadened at the mouth, and jagged rocks formed the riverbed. Here the breakers crashed in from the open sea, and anything pushed further would be dashed against the rocks. But the current lessened slightly—almost imperceptibly—just before the rocks.

Man and woman kicked fiercely in unison, and they reached the shore just as the first of the rocks came into view.

Even then they didn't have the joey safe. As they staggered to their feet in shallow water they were confronted by a sandy cliff reaching five or six feet up from the river-bed. There was nothing to hold.

'Now what?' Jackson managed a rueful grin at the predicament they were facing. He was lifting the bundle high out of the water, but already the 'roo was starting to struggle free.

'You go up and I'll push,' Molly told him.

'You're kidding?'

'Nope.'

'I have a better idea.' He rewrapped the 'roo until he was sure those claws couldn't come free and handed the whole thing to Molly. He hauled himself in against the cliff and cupped his hands so she could use them as a step.

'Up you go.'

She looked at Jackson and looked at the cliff. 'I can't.'

'Of course you can, girl,' he said equitably. 'After all, there's no choice—so what choice do you have?'

Somehow their crazy scheme worked. Somehow Molly was propelled upwards to land in a laughing sodden heap on the grassy verge. Then she reached down to grab Jackson's hand as he hauled himself up. He came in a rush and almost landed on top of her—a soggy ball of 'roo, man and woman.

And they were safe.

'We've done it,' Molly gasped as Jackson untied their bundle of baby 'roo.

Yes. They'd done the thing. Jackson looked down at her and his mouth twisted in a rueful smile. She was battered and soggy and exhausted. She was limp with relief. And he'd never seen anything more beautiful...

'He's gorgeous,' Molly murmured as the blanket fell away from the sodden joey.

The baby 'roo did look gorgeous. Kind of. But then, so did the girl. With a huge effort Jackson managed a response. 'Yeah, right. Gorgeous. But stupid.' The joey was shaking its head in disbelief. They'd landed on the opposite bank from where they'd started—on the same bank as the joey's mother—and already the mother 'roo was peering towards them, trying to see what was happening.

'Stupid! What a thing to say!'

'I'm a pragmatist,' he retorted. 'Someone has to be. If I wasn't a pragmatist you'd have tried to rescue the joey without a rug, and you'd be bleeding to death right now.'

She managed a grin, albeit a shaky one. 'Then I'm glad you're a pragmatist. But I'm also… Oh, Jackson, he's going to jump!'

'Mmm.'

Her eyes narrowed. 'Are you okay?'

Suddenly he *was* okay. More than okay. He felt great. They'd struggled against the odds and they'd won, and it was as far from the everyday white-collar wheeling and dealing as he'd been for years. His eyes met Molly's and they were full of laughter and of triumph. 'Oh, well done. Well done us.'

'Jackson…'

There was no need for more. He heard the warning in her voice and turned to see the mother 'roo thundering down from along the bank. The 'roo had seen her baby and was now taking steps to get him back.

'Give him a push away,' Molly urged, half-laughing, half-serious. These 'roos were big! Bull kangaroos were dangerous enough, but to stand between a 'roo and her joey…

'I'm trying.' Jackson grabbed the blanket and lifted it away—and then retreated. Fast.

Freedom...

The joey gave one more unbelieving shake of his head, he reared on wobbly legs—and then took off for his mother as if Molly and Jackson were the cause of all his problems rather than his saviours.

'Well, will you look at that?' But Jackson was grinning with a smile that almost split his face. The joey had reached his mother. The 'roo nosed him all over and then the joey dived straight down, deep into his mother's pouch. The 'roo took off before the joey's legs had disappeared, and gave the strange humans not so much as a backward glance as they headed for the safety of the mob. 'That's gratitude for you.'

'I'm grateful,' Molly said before she could stop herself—because she was. She couldn't have saved the joey herself. Maybe it had been dangerous to try, but there'd been too much death in her life over the last few months. If she could stop just one death...

'You know, you can't save the world.' He was watching her face and guessing what she was thinking.

She flushed. 'I can try.'

'Molly...' And then, before he even knew what he intended, he reached for her.

Why? He hardly knew. But she was so alone. Kneeling on the sandy bank, watching the 'roo with worried eyes that still reflected her fear of unnecessary death... She was sodden and bruised and shaken and there was suddenly no choice but to take her in his arms. To hold her hard against him so her breasts moulded to his chest.

To comfort...

No. This was more than comfort. This was need! He could feel her heart beating against his and it felt right. He kissed the top of her head, and when she raised her face to him in mute enquiry it was entirely natural that his hold became tighter. It felt right that his mouth should lower onto hers…

He kissed her. Of course he kissed her. And what a kiss! She tasted of salt—of the sea. She tasted of…

Of what? He didn't know. All he knew was that this was a kiss such as he'd never experienced.

He'd kissed so many soft, pliant, lipsticked mouths that pursed into perfectly formed kisses and claimed him as their right. But there was no cool expertise here.

Their first touch fell awry, as if she hadn't expected it—wasn't wanting it—didn't know what to do with it when she received it.

But she didn't pull away. Her response was almost wondering. As if she didn't understand that she was being kissed. Didn't understand why.

And she wanted nothing from it but the touch. She needed comfort. She needed reassurance that here was life in the face of death. That she'd tried and she'd won and here was the man who had helped her achieve it. And he was solid and strong and male and wonderful…

She asked for nothing more. Her hands came up to take his face in her palms and her lips parted under his. Welcoming the kiss. Deepening. Glorying in the triumph of the moment—of the triumph of him—of the triumph of life itself!

The sun was warm on their sea-soaked bodies. With every moment they were recovering. Soon they'd surface to sanity, but until then they took each other in a desperate hunger that had nothing to do with the courting rituals each was accustomed to. Here was a man and a woman, and the sun and the sand, and the world around them was a mere backdrop to their need.

And when finally they pulled apart—as pull apart they must, though neither wanted it—there was no confusion between them. Only a deep assurance that it had been right. The right place. The right time. The right man for the right woman.

There was laughter in Molly's eyes—not the carefully rehearsed confusion he'd come to expect from the women who saw his money coming before he did. There was no false coyness here. She was laughing at him and she was reaching up to touch his hair.

'You're wearing a crown of seaweed, King Neptune.'

'Ditto for you.' He lifted a strand from her shoulder and tossed it aside. 'Hell. We must look like...'

'Shipwreck victims?' She was still laughing, glorying in the moment. 'But for what better reason? Oh, Jackson, wasn't that marvellous?'

'Marvellous,' he agreed, and he couldn't agree more.

Her eyes were dancing with joy. 'Want to do it again?'

'I suspect our kangaroo won't be *that* stupid!'

'Was I talking about the 'roo?' But she chuckled, letting him off the hook. 'Okay. I was talking about the 'roo.' She'd pulled right back from him and was hauling up the leg of her jeans. 'And I definitely don't want to do that again. I hit my leg on a stump as I came up the bank. Look at the size of this bruise!'

Damn, it was as if the kiss had never happened. Despite himself Jackson couldn't help feeling a little piqued. After all, he had kissed the girl. He wasn't accustomed to kissing a woman and having no reaction at all.

Especially when the kiss had felt so perfect.

It was because it was the result of triumph, he told himself. Nothing more. It was the emotion of the moment. Molly would know as well as he did that the kiss could mean nothing—that they'd move back to business from this point on.

So keep it light, he told himself. Despite the fact that he quite suddenly—quite desperately—wanted to reach for her again. Wanted to take her in his arms again…

'I have matching bruises,' he told her, and only he knew what an effort it was to keep his voice light.

'Can I see?'

That brought a laugh. 'Nope. They're in places a good realtor shouldn't look.'

'Uncharted territory, eh?'

'Something like that.' They were grinning at each other like fools, and then the tension sprang back and he didn't know what the hell to do with it. Because he couldn't kiss her again—could he?

No. He couldn't. Not without starting something he couldn't stop. Because having a light flirtation with Molly Farr…

No! The thing was impossible, and he didn't know why. It would be like starting a wild fire, he thought. He wouldn't know how to put it out or even if he'd want to.

What was he thinking of? Of course he'd want to put it out. Had he learned nothing over the last few months? Hadn't he and Cara made a pact? No relationship with anyone they could fall in love with—that was the deal.

He shook his head as if dispelling a dream, then managed a smile at Molly as he hauled himself to his feet. He held out a hand to help her to hers.

She looked at the hand for a long moment, then placed hers in his. It was as if she was coming to some sort of decision. Her hand in his felt warm and strong and sure—and…right?

Yeah. Pigs might fly, he told himself harshly. Right? Hardly. Wrong and wrong and wrong.

'We'd best get back to the house,' he managed, and she smiled up at him as if she was unaware of the tumult of emotions running through his head. He looked across the river, concentrating on anything but Molly, and found something there to concentrate on. 'Oh, hell. Your horse is gone. You mustn't have tethered it.'

'Then we go back fast. She'll head to the homestead unbridled and start a panic.'

'And that would never do.'

'I won't scare Sam,' she said bluntly, and started walking back along the bank to where the river narrowed and it would be quicker to swim across.

He fell in by her side, his pique increasing by the minute. He wasn't accustomed to being treated as this woman was treating him. 'But you'll jump into the river to save a kangaroo and risk drowning yourself into the bargain? How does that equate with not scaring Sam?'

She stopped then and turned back to him, responding to the note of anger in his voice with bewilderment. 'I was never in danger. If I couldn't have saved the 'roo I would have swum back.'

'And if the current had been too strong?'

'You know very well the river broadens at the mouth. The water becomes shallower and the current less strong. If I'd been in danger of going past the point of no return I could have swum back before I reached the rocks.'

'Damn, Molly, you could have died.'

'I couldn't. Don't make me out to be some sort of heroine.'

'Isn't that what you are?' Still there was anger in his voice, and he couldn't figure it out himself. 'Doing rugby tackles to save a frog? Leaping into the breach to save a drowning 'roo? Taking on an orphan—'

'Don't do this.' There was no mistaking her matching anger. It was blazing from her brown eyes, slashing at him with fury. 'I took in Sam for me. *Me.* Sure, Sam needs me. But I need him, too. I lost my sister and my brother-in-law and my way of life. I don't have anyone but Sam. I took Sam in for me—if you want to cast anyone as a heroine then go find yourself a storybook damsel, but don't pick on me. I'm not it.'

'I—'

'And don't think I'll fall trembling into your arms like good heroines should,' she threw at him before he could recover.

'I never thought that.'

She forestalled him. 'So why did you kiss me?'

'Hey, it wasn't just me. You kissed me back.'

Her hands were on her hips, her curls were sodden and awry, there was still a streak of seaweed in her hair—and again he thought he'd never seen anything so beautiful. 'I might have kissed you, but I didn't mean it,' she snapped. 'I was cold.'

'You *were* trembling.'

'So were you.'

That made his eyebrows rise. 'Me? Tremble?'

'Yes.' Her grin surfaced, anger receding. 'You were definitely trembling. So there, Mr Hero Baird. Heroes shake, too.'

The woman was incorrigible. 'I did not shake.'

'You did, and I couldn't have you dying of shock. It'd do me all sorts of damage.'

'Worried you'll lose a valuable client?'

'Certainly I am. I've told you. Trevor would kill me if I

brought you back dead. So that's the only reason I kissed back.'

'Yeah, right.'

There was nothing else to say. They slithered down the riverbank into the water and struck out for the opposite shore, side by side.

There was still this intimacy between them. It was unbelievably intimate to swim with her, matching stroke for stroke. It was sort of…two becoming one.

Which was crazy…

Then they gained the point where one horse still stayed tethered. They reached for their boots and he looked doubtfully down at them. At last: a topic of conversation that wasn't fraught with tension.

'My socks are squelchy.'

'I'm taking mine off.' She sat on the riverbank and proceeded to do just that, then swivelled to find him watching her with a very odd expression on his face. 'What? Haven't you seen bare feet before?'

He had. Of course he had. And why the sight of a sodden Molly hauling off even more sodden socks had his insides turning handsprings he didn't know. All he knew was that it did.

'Unimaginably erotic,' he murmured, and she gave one of her lovely low chuckles.

'That's me. Mata Hari has nothing on me. Dance of the seven veils be damned. This is the saga of two soggy socks.' She raised her eyebrows at him. 'You're not joining me?'

'In a striptease? I hardly think so.' He sat and hauled his boots over his socks regardless, and she looked at him in astonishment.

'There's modesty and there's modesty. And then there's plain stupidity. You know, I won't faint if I see bare toes.'

'No, but my boots will feel like the very devil on bare skin.'

'You don't have to walk. Your horse is still here—mine's bolted!'

'You can ride mine.'

She grinned again. 'What a hero. Thank you very much, but, no. Not me.'

'Why ever not?'

'And have you tell Trevor I made a client walk? Not on your life. I know what my job's worth.'

'I won't tell Trevor anything of the kind. Of course you'll ride.'

'Of course I won't.'

'Then we'll both walk.'

'That's ridiculous.'

'Ridiculous or not, that's the way it is.'

# CHAPTER FIVE

So HALF an hour later Gregor came out of the yard to find a sodden Molly and Jackson trudging up to the house, their one horse walking easily between them. The frown on Gregor's old face lightened. The mare had indeed come home, and the sight of her had shaken him badly. He hadn't told Doreen—he hadn't wanted to worry her—but he'd been about to get on the farm bike, regardless of his bad hip, and go and find out what the damage was.

However, there was apparently no damage at all. They were walking easily. The girl was laughing. Even the horse looked undamaged. But why weren't they riding him...?

'Did we scare you?' Molly called, and his trouble receded even further. There was no problem behind that light, lovely laughter.

'No, miss. Well, yes you did a bit. I didn't like to see the mare come home without you. I thought you must have come off over a bump.'

'No such thing. I didn't tether her right.'

'We stopped to rescue a joey that had fallen in the river,' Jackson added, but his eyes were on Molly. She had him fascinated. She still looked crazy. Soaking and tumbled and sanded like the coating on a rissole. Cara would die if she was seen like this, he thought suddenly. Cara and every other woman who moved in his circles. But Molly seemed not to even notice.

'Sam wasn't worried?' she asked, and the old man shook his head.

'I didn't tell him. No use spreading trouble before you need to.'

'Very wise.'

'The 'roo?'

'Tried to cross the river on a bunch of leaf litter that wasn't the least bit stable.'

'Hell. I know where that'll have happened.' Gregor nodded. 'It's happened before. I lost a calf that way once. Things wedge in that bend in the river.' He grimaced. 'It ought to be checked every day.' His face set, as if expecting a blow.

Molly knew what he was thinking. If Jackson bought the place Gregor would hardly have recommended himself as a future farm manager. But he didn't try to absolve himself from responsibility. He braced himself and confessed all. 'I didn't do the rounds this morning, and I should have.'

'You're the only full-time man on the place?' Jackson asked slowly, and Molly watched Gregor's face fall even further. Here we go, she thought. Jackson's going to suggest retirement.

'Yes.' Gregor took the bay's rein and Molly saw his shoulders go back into brace position. Waiting for the inevitable.

It didn't come.

'According to the title there's two smaller houses on the property.' Jackson was still frowning. 'I assume you and Doreen have one?'

'Yes. The caretaker's cottage.'

'And the other?'

'It's empty.'

'But it's liveable?'

'Oh, yes, sir,' Gregor told him. 'It's a nice little place,

overlooking the bay to the south of the river. Time was when the farm manager lived there.'

'This place *has* a farm manager,' Jackson said briefly. 'You. But it needs more. A place of this size can't prosper with casual labour. It needs permanents. What you need is a solid young man you could gradually train to take over as you ease back. Or a couple. What would you say to doing some training?'

'You mean training them and then leaving?'

'I don't mean anything of the sort,' Jackson said curtly. 'If I buy I'll need all the expertise I can get, and losing the people who know most about the place would be stupid. There'd be work here for you and Doreen for as long as you want, and even in retirement I'd want you to stay on as advisers.'

It was as if the sun had come out. 'Do you mean it?' Gregor sounded incredulous.

'I haven't bought the place yet,' Jackson warned him. 'But, yes. If I do buy then I mean it.'

The man's breath came out in a rush as he heaved a great sigh of relief. 'Then it's up to me and Doreen to see you buy,' he said simply. 'You go inside and see what Doreen's been cooking. Maybe that'll push you into making the right choice.'

The sun had come out for Molly as well. It was as if it had been some sort of test—and Jackson had passed with flying colours.

If Jackson needed more persuasion, Doreen had just the means to persuade.

Pavlova. Swiss roll. Pikelets, fresh from the oven. Gem scones. Molly stopped at the kitchen door and blinked in astonishment as she took in the lavish spread.

'Come and see what we've made.' Sam beamed from the business side of a mixing bowl of truly gigantic proportions—a bowl that had been well and truly licked. 'Mrs Gray's the world's bestest cook.'

'I can see that she is,' Molly said, and looked sideways at Jackson. If ever there was a sales pitch that would work, this was it. It had been ages since lunch, the swim had sharpened their appetite, and the smells were just...

'Fantastic,' Jackson said, and he grinned at Doreen and then at Sam. 'Did you help make all of this?'

He was seeming nicer and nicer, Molly thought happily, and had to catch herself. She was moving too fast here, and in the wrong direction. This man was a client. Nothing more.

'I rolled up the Swiss roll,' Sam said importantly. 'And I dropped the batter for the pikelets into the pan all by myself.' Then he paused in his bowl-licking and stared at the pair of them, noting their discreditable appearance for the first time. 'Have you been swimming?'

'Yes,' Molly said swiftly, with a warning glance at Jackson.

Sam's face fell. 'Without me?'

'You don't like swimming.' She'd tried him once before and it had been a disaster.

But... 'I might,' Sam said cautiously. 'With Mr Baird.'

So Sam was being sucked into this man's charismatic presence as well. Well, it was dangerous territory for Sam as well as Molly! 'Mr Baird has business to keep him occupied, Sam.'

'Mr Baird?' Sam turned pleading eyes to Jackson. Swimming could hardly be any fun without him, his eyes said. And who could resist an appeal like that?

Jackson grinned and capitulated, tugging Molly's heart-strings even further from their rightful position. 'Of course I'll take you swimming,' he told him. 'But not until I've done justice to what's in front of me.' He sat and hauled over the plate of gem scones. 'I haven't had a gem scone since I was six. Mrs Gray, you're a gem yourself.'

'Get on with you,' the woman said, beaming, and for some inexplicable reason Molly suddenly felt like weeping. She didn't feel like a realtor here. She felt like an angel of fate, putting this farm together with the man who was meant to call it home. And putting Jackson alongside... alongside Sam? And her?

The thought made her catch her breath in sudden panic. Jackson looked up from his gem scone and his eyes met Molly's. And held...

'We've found a friend for Lionel,' Sam announced, un-aware of the emotional currents running deep between man and woman.

Molly tried to move her gaze, but couldn't. It was like a magnetic pull. A vast magnetic pull. 'For...for Lionel?' The words had to be dragged out.

'My frog,' Sam said with patience, and Molly nodded. Of course. She knew that.

It was just that she was being temporarily distracted, she thought wildly. Jackson was munching his gem scone as he watched her. His shirt was undone down to the fourth button, there was dark hair wisping on his chest, his grey eyes were deep and fathomless and faintly questioning—as if he didn't know what was going on either—and the sight of him...

Lionel. Right. Lionel. Concentrate on the frog!

'You've found a friend for Lionel?' She lifted a slice of Swiss roll to hide her confusion, took a bite and promptly choked. Jackson grinned, rose, and came around to thump her on the back—which did exactly nothing for her equilibrium. The rat! It was as if he knew how much he was unsettling her.

'Mr Gray took me down to the dam at the back of the house,' Sam told her, his small-boy patience tested to the limit by these stupid adults. 'Mr Gray says Lionel's a green tree frog or a lit…litoria something and he's a boy. And we searched and searched and we found a girl frog! A girl green tree frog! Mr Gray says we should keep the lady frog until Lionel's better, so he won't be lonely, and then we should bring them both back here. So they can have tadpoles and live happily ever after.'

'That's…' All at once Molly was close to tears again. This man! This place! The whole damned package! 'That's wonderful. But…'

'But what?'

Somehow she made herself think it through. And found a flaw. 'I don't think you'll be coming here again,' she said gently, and watched a mulish expression settle on her nephew's face.

'Of course I will. Mr and Mrs Gray are my friends, and Mr Baird will buy the farm and he's my friend, too.'

'Sam—'

'I tell you what,' Jackson said, watching the interplay between woman and child with interest. Dispassionate interest, he told himself. But he was starting to wonder if he knew what the word dispassionate meant. 'If you don't come back, what if I make a special trip to release Mr and Mrs Frog?'

Molly's jaw dropped about a foot. 'You'd make a special trip—to release two frogs?' Her voice was about an octave too high.

'They're special frogs,' Jackson said equitably. 'And

didn't you know the frog population is endangered world-wide? Any small mite I can do to help their numbers rise…'

'You know, you stand in real danger of losing your reputation,' she retorted, and his eyes quizzed hers with mocking laughter.

'What—as a womaniser?'

She frowned him down on that one. 'I mean as a ruthless businessman.'

He was still laughing. 'So I can keep being a womaniser?'

'You can keep being whatever you want.' She pushed herself to her feet. There were undercurrents here that she didn't understand in the least, and she was almost being swept out of her depth. Those laughing eyes were dangerous. Womaniser? Yes and yes and yes. She had to preserve her dignity—and sanity—at all costs.

'I'm taking a bath,' she told him.

He rose as well, and grinned. 'Me, too.'

Heck, she was feeling so darn crowded she didn't know what to think. 'I dare say there are two bathrooms.'

'There are four,' Doreen said promptly, and Molly managed a smile.

'There you go, then.' She managed to smile sweetly at him, businesswoman dismissing client nicely. 'And I dare say you need to spend some time with Gregor and the farm books before dinner.'

He did. Damnably, he did.

'I thought you might like to take a barbecue to the beach for dinner,' Doreen volunteered. 'Being as it's such a lovely evening.'

'I'm sure Mr Baird will be far too busy—'

'Too busy for a barbecue on the beach?' Jackson interrupted, and shook his head, his eyes glinting a challenge at her. 'Never. Shall we meet here again in...?' He glanced at his watch. 'In two hours, Miss Farr?'

It was as if he was asking her for a date. His eyes were challenging, gently mocking, and it took all her self-control to keep a straight face.

'Fine.'

'You don't sound excited.'

'I'm excited,' she said through clenched teeth. 'I'm so excited I can hardly speak.'

'Very good.' He reached out and touched her cheek with his finger—a feather touch—a tease and no more—and it had no business to pack the electric charge that it did. 'You stay excited, then, Miss Farr. Until dinner.'

Yeah, right. What else was she supposed to do?

Time out. That was what this was, Molly thought as she lay neck-deep in bath suds. Sam had no intention of being dislodged from the kitchen—he'd decided the elderly Grays were the nearest thing to heaven that a small boy could imagine, and they in turn thought Sam was the cat's pyjamas. For Sam and the Grays it had been love at first sight, Molly thought reflectively. She wiped a soap bubble off her nose and thought, What about her?

Love at first sight?

Hardly. What was she thinking of? She'd only known the man for two days.

Oh, for heaven's sake—she wasn't in love. She wasn't! Sure, he was drop-dead gorgeous, and he certainly seemed to be turning on the charm—turning it up to full throttle!—but the man was an international jetsetter and he'd been seen with more gorgeous women than she could count.

But he was kind. And people could change. Just because

he'd dated some of the world's most glamorous women it didn't mean that he had to marry someone like that.

Hold on just a second, she told herself abruptly. Where was she going here?

Marry?

She was living in a soap bubble, she told herself and grinned, held her nose and sank right under the water. And don't come up 'til you've seen sense, she told herself—only to emerge spluttering thirty seconds later knowing that she wasn't seeing sense at all.

This might be a soap bubble she was indulging in, but it was a very nice soap bubble.

You're being stupid. He's dangerous, she warned herself.

*He could be fun, and heaven knows you need a bit of fun. After Sarah's death and Michael's treachery... Life's been too bleak lately,* the more daring part of her argued.

And if he breaks your heart? questioned the cautious part.

*He can only break your heart if you give it to him for the breaking. And you're not a fool. Enjoy this, Molly Farr, and then move on.*

Hmm.

It'd be walking a very fine line, she thought, to let herself enjoy his company and relax and have fun, then walk away at the end heart-whole and fancy-free. But she must. The man was a client.

'Yes, and it's back to business from now on,' she muttered. 'One kiss does not a relationship make.'

But one kiss did make for interest—and she was definitely interested.

And Jackson? He sat with Gregor and went through the farm figures, but only half his mind was on what he was doing—which was very unusual for him. Usually where business was concerned his mind was like a steel trap, letting nothing escape. Now... The figures looked good, he thought. Very good. He knew he could do what he wanted with this farm, but if Gregor had wanted to pull the wool over his eyes then maybe he'd have let it happen.

Because half his mind was on Molly. Half? Well, maybe more than half.

Why?

And that was the major question. He didn't know. Sure, she was attractive. Sure, she had a gorgeous chuckle—but he'd been with some of the most beautiful women in the world and beside them Molly didn't rate.

Or didn't she? She certainly had *something,* and when he'd kissed her that something had nearly blown him apart.

But he'd been blown apart before. Almost. And he had no intention of letting it happen again, he told himself determinedly. He had the life he wanted—and he had no room in that life for a frog-loving realtor and her kid. They'd need things he had no intention—no capability—of giving.

'Mr Gray? Mr Baird?' Sam stood in the doorway, his frog box clutched to his stomach, and both men looked around.

'Yes?' said Gregor, and smiled—an old man smile that made Sam relax a bit and edge into the room. He talked to Gregor but his eyes slid sideways to Jackson.

'If Mr Baird buys the farm, will he keep the frogs here safe?'

'Of course I will,' Jackson said, nettled, and Sam cast him a doubtful look, as if there was no *of course* about it.

'Mrs Gray says the prettiest place on the farm is the frog dam—but she said the last people Mrs Copeland thought about selling the farm to wanted to make the dam a whole lot bigger. They had surveyors and everything, and Miss Copeland got so angry she decided not to sell. Mrs Gray said she was so relieved that she cried.' He fixed Jackson with a look. 'But that was five years ago now, so me and Mrs Gray want to know...'

So Hannah had thought about selling the place before, had she? Jackson thought, trying to make sense of this. A gap of five years between tries, though, meant she was hardly rushing her sale. And enlarging the dam? That made sense, too. The house dam was small, and if there was a hot summer then water would have to be pumped from the lower levels. That'd be expensive.

But he'd been thrown a challenge and Sam was still watching.

'Do you think Miss Copeland wouldn't want me to buy the farm if I want to enlarge the dam?'

'Mrs Gray says the frogs would die. She said the bulldozer would take out all the reeds and without the reeds they couldn't breed.'

They were measuring each other up—Jackson and Sam—with Gregor a spectator at the side.

'Do you think I should buy the farm?' Jackson asked, and Sam considered.

'Yes. Mrs Gray thinks you'd be good. But we're both worried about the frogs.'

'So?'

'So make us a promise about the frogs and buy the farm.'

And he made a decision. Figures or not. Sense or not. 'Okay,' he said. 'I will.'

'He says he's going to buy the farm!' Molly was still nose-deep in bath suds but Sam wasn't waiting. This news was too important, and he burst into the bathroom almost shouting. 'He's going to save the frogs and live here for ever and ever!'

'Did he say that?' Molly sat up and grabbed her towel. The bath suds were making her decent, but only just. Luckily Sam had no concept of her as a woman—he thought of her only as his Aunty Molly. He didn't even notice that, apart from suds, she was stark naked.

'Yes.'

'Are you sure?'

'He definitely promised.' Sam was standing in the doorway, still clutching his frog box, and now he raised his voice to call someone in the distance. To Molly's horror, it was Jackson. 'Mr Baird, come and tell Aunty Molly that you're buying the farm.'

'No! Sam, no!' Molly gasped, and tried to tell him to close the door—but it was too late. Jackson must have been walking down the passage as Sam had called. Now he appeared above Sam, so man and child were framed in the bathroom door, both gazing at her with very different levels of interest.

Jackson's gaze found her under the soap suds and his grey eyes glinted with wicked laughter. But his voice, when he finally spoke, was deadpan.

'Miss Farr, I believe I'd like to formally let it be known that I'd like to buy the farm,' he said.

Molly took a deep breath and took a firmer grasp on her towel. It was covering the important bits—just—which left her free to concentrate on what had to be the major issue here. A sale. 'You mean it?'

'Why wouldn't I mean it?'

'You agree to the asking price?' She wasn't letting a bit of false modesty get in the way of a sale, and Jackson's laughter deepened.

'Yes. You want to stand up and shake on it?'

'In your dreams.' She glared at him. 'You realise I don't have Miss Copeland's conditions yet?'

'Neither do I, and of course it's dependent on those, but I gather there are frogs.'

She looked uncertainly at Jackson, and then at Sam. 'Do you know what he's talking about?' she demanded of her nephew.

'I know Miss Copeland cares about frogs,' Sam told her. 'And Mr Baird says he'll save the frogs.'

Oh, for heaven's sake! She was trying to keep a grip on the situation and they were discussing frogs! She was trying to sound businesslike, which for a girl who was depending on soap suds was rather tricky. 'Right. But let's assume there are to be other stipulations. I need to find out.' She chanced another uncertain look at Jackson. She was very much at a disadvantage here—realtor in bathtub.

Realtor stark naked!

But if she was out of control Jackson was very much in control—and enjoying himself hugely. 'So what are you waiting for?' He was cordiality itself. He folded his arms and leaned against the doorjamb, his eyes gleaming. 'Sitting round in bathtubs when you could be wrapping up a sale…'

'Go away!'

'Go away?' His eyebrows hit his hairline. 'You want me to tell Trevor that when I asked to sign a contract you told me to go away?'

'I don't have the contract in the bathroom with me.' She was fighting for her dignity for all she was worth.

'You sure you don't have it hidden on your person?'

That was a bit much. The man had no shame! 'It'd be pretty soggy if it was,' she retorted, and he grinned—and kept right on grinning. He put a hand on Sam's shoulder. They stood, man and boy, laughing down at her, and Molly's insides twisted as they hadn't been twisted for a long, long time.

Sam was leaning back into the man behind him, and the little boy seemed to be relishing the hand on his shoulder— the intimacy of his aunt in the bath and this man taking a proprietary role. This man was exactly what Sam needed, Molly thought, and then she thought, This man is exactly what *I* need...

'You know, those suds are disappearing,' Jackson said kindly. 'You must have been using soap. Bath foam always disappears when you use soap.'

Molly gave a squeak of indignation and clutched at her towel as if her life depended on it. She could use another six inches of towelling here. Badly. 'Sam, take Mr Baird out and close the door after you.'

'We're comfortable here,' Sam said. He grinned and his aunt moaned.

'Sam, don't you dare turn into another machiavellian male before my eyes. I depend on you.'

'That's why we're staying.' Jackson grinned. 'Because you depend on us.'

'I don't depend on *you*.'

'You hear that, Sam? And that's about a man she's hoping to make a sale to.'

'Get out.' Molly was caught between laughter and exasperation. And something else. Jackson was engendering a feeling she hadn't known she was capable of. The way he held Sam. The way he laughed down at her...

'Get out,' she said again, and her eyes locked on his and held.

A message passed between them.

A message?

No. It was more than that. It was a forging of a link, Molly thought faintly, and that link she didn't fully understand, but it was a link for all that. Strong and warm and...

'Get out,' she said again, but this time it was more than that. Get out—and she wasn't just talking about leaving the bathroom.

This man was starting to alarm her.

Starting? Ha!

And Jackson? He stood staring down at her for a long minute, and very gradually the laughter died from his eyes. Finally he nodded, and it was as if he'd come to a decision.

'Right,' he said. 'We know when we're not wanted.' And he turned and walked back down the passage without a backward glance.

By the time she'd dressed and dried her hair she almost had herself under control. Almost. Molly was badly flustered and it showed. She blew dry her hair and didn't concentrate, so she had to do it again—it was that or wear an unruly mop for dinner. Even when she wet and reblew it, her curls still flew everywhere.

No matter. It didn't matter. Did it?

No. She dressed in jeans and a clean shirt, then changed her mind and donned a skirt—then went back to jeans. By the time she finished she was thoroughly disconcerted, and Sam was asking questions.

'Why is it taking you so long? Don't you know Mr Baird is waiting?'

It was exactly because Mr Baird was waiting that she was taking so long, Molly thought. She gave her curls a last despairing brush and headed for the kitchen, Sam skipping by her side.

Because, yes, Mr Baird was waiting.

To her dismay Doreen and Gregor had no intention of joining them for their barbecue.

'Gregor hates sand,' Doreen told them, casting an affectionate glance at her husband. 'You'd think after forty years of living at the beach he'd grow accustomed to it.'

'I'll never get accustomed to sand,' Gregor said morosely. 'Foul stuff gets everywhere. You even find it between your toes!'

'Don't you like sand between your toes?' Sam asked, his eyes falling to Gregor's severely laced boots. The vision of Gregor's old toes was somehow fascinating and repelling all at once.

'Don't tell me you do?' Gregor demanded. 'Well! There's no accounting for taste. But that's why Doreen's packed you a hamper of everything you might fancy to eat on sand while I eat my dinner at the kitchen table like a gentleman.'

And that was that. They were, it seemed, dining on the beach alone. Just Molly and Jackson and Sam.

Great, thought Molly, and...help?

But the setting itself was magic. At any other time Molly would have loved it. The sun was sinking over the mountains, the surf was rolling in long, low swells onto the wide ribbon of beach, and the sand was still warm from the heat of the day. Gregor had been down before them and had lit a fire.

'Main course is a nice piece of beef I've buried in the coals, and there's spuds down there as well,' he told them. 'Just dig when you get hungry.'

Or eat the rest of their food? They could certainly do

that. The appetisers alone would have satisfied even the hungriest of diners. Doreen had done them proud. They unpacked onto the picnic rug and discovered prawns on ice, and scallops and oysters in their shells. There were tiny sausage rolls, still warm. Delicate sandwiches, asparagus, chicken and avocado, smoked salmon...

And the sweets...

'And this after morning tea, lunch and afternoon tea... The Grays must think we starve in our other lives,' Molly said, awed, and Jackson grinned and reached for a prawn.

'Who's complaining? Sausage roll, Sam? Lemonade? Champagne, Miss Farr?'

'There's four different types of wine.' Molly was practically dumbfounded. 'How did they do this?'

'Mrs Gray rang up some people while you were out today,' Sam told her. 'They delivered stuff.'

They certainly must have. 'You'll have to push me home in a wheelbarrow if I wrap myself round this lot.' She shook her head as Jackson offered her wine. 'I'll have lemonade, please.'

'You're not scared things might get out of control?' he asked, gently teasing, and she flushed.

'No. But I'm careful.'

'Because of my reputation?'

'I hardly think you'll try a spot of seduction with Sam here,' Molly snapped, and she got what she asked for.

'What's seduction?' asked Sam.

'Making ladies kiss you when they should know better,' she told him. Her response was out before she could stop herself, and there was a crack of laughter from Jackson.

'That means your Aunty Molly would really, really like to kiss me but she thinks she's too respectable.'

'Is that why she changed three times before she decided

what to wear tonight?' Sam asked, interested in this weird adult behaviour, and Molly was torn between embarrassment and laughter.

Suddenly laughter won. Well, why not? It was either laugh or blush to the roots of her hair, and Jackson had the upper hand already.

'Hand me a sausage roll,' she told Sam. 'I'm missing out on valuable eating time talking about stupid things like kissing.'

'I thought girls liked kissing.' Sam was looking from Jackson to Molly and back again, trying to figure things out for himself. 'You mean you don't want to kiss each other?'

'What, kiss Mr Baird? Why on earth would I want to kiss Mr Baird?'

Sam thought that one through and found it a reasonable question.

'Well, I wouldn't want to. But some people might.'

'Kissing's dangerous. You've read your fairy stories. Jackson could turn into a frog.'

'Or a prince.'

'Not a prince,' Molly said decisively. 'Millionaires don't turn into princes. They always turn into frogs. It's in the rules.'

'But we like frogs.'

'A frog called Jackson? I don't think so. And besides, it'd be a toad.'

'Thanks very much,' Jackson said drily.

'You're welcome.' Molly gave him her sweetest smile. 'Now, Sam, I suggest we shut up and eat. Otherwise we might go hungry.'

'What, with all this?'

'And afternoon tea was so puny,' Molly agreed mournfully. 'I'm starving to my socks.'

Sam gave up the kissing issue as a bad job and giggled, a cheerful small boy sound that added to the impression of magic that was all around them. He'd laughed so little since his parents died, and here he was wolfing down sausage rolls and spreading his toes in the sand—and leaning back against Jackson, for heaven's sake, almost as if he belonged there.

'Me, too,' he said cheerfully, munching his fourth sausage roll and giving a direct lie to his statement. 'Mr Baird, are you starving to your socks?'

'Deeper,' Jackson said with aplomb. 'I'm starving to my toenails.'

# CHAPTER SIX

IT WAS a magic meal. A magic night. They ate their fill and then took Sam down for a paddle in the shallows. The child had spent very little time at the beach in his life. Despite Jackson's reassuring presence he was still wary of the water, so Jackson and Molly held him between them and did one-two-three-jumps over the waves until they were all exhausted.

And wet.

'Why didn't we wear our bathers?' Molly demanded as they paused for breath. 'Look at us. Sam, you're wet up to your neck.'

'Speaking of swimming—Sam, how do you feel about having a shot at real swimming tomorrow?' Jackson asked him, adult to adult. 'I'd be pleased to show you how.'

Molly held her breath as Sam perused Jackson's face, but what he saw there seemed to reassure him.

'That would be good.'

*That would be good...* Understatement of the year! Molly let her breath out in a rush and felt like singing or dancing or... Or she knew what. She let out a war whoop of triumph and did a pirouette in the shallows, spinning round and round and round while Jackson and Sam looked on as if she'd lost her marbles.

'You know, she doesn't look like any businesswoman I've ever met,' Jackson told Sam gravely, and Sam nodded.

'She's not really a businesswoman. She's just my aunty Molly.'

And that felt good, too, Molly thought. *My aunty Molly.*

It was a claim of ownership, and Sam had never made that before either. She whooped across to him, seized him in her arms and spun him round with her until they were both dizzy and sank laughing in the shallows. Then they looked up...

To find Jackson with a very strange expression on his face. One Molly couldn't read at all.

'What?' she said crossly, and he caught himself and managed a grin.

'Nothing. I was just thinking.'

'Don't tell me. You were thinking how unsuitable I am to sell you a farm?'

'Not at all,' he said, and his grin deepened. 'What I was really thinking was that if we tried I bet we could make the world's biggest sandcastle. How about making a frog— right here on the beach?'

'A frog?' Sam was sitting on his aunt's knee while the waves washed over him, flushed and happy and game. 'How do you make a frog?'

'Out of sand. Watch. And help. I've been involved in several great construction companies in my time. How about if I declare us the Molly, Sam & Jackson Construction Company Ltd, and we start building forthwith?'


And they did. An hour later there was a frog, four feet wide and almost as high, sitting up on his haunches regarding them all with frog-like eyes made of shells and the blandest of seaweedy smiles.

'He looks like he wants to eat us all for breakfast,' Molly said, sitting back and admiring her handiwork. 'Oh, Jackson, he's wonderful.'

It wasn't just the frog that was wonderful, she thought, dazed with happiness. It was the whole night. Sam was by her side and she sank back on the sand and let him fall into the crook of her arm. The little boy was close to sleep. He was happier on this night than he'd been since the night his parents had been killed, and he was smiling up at them through closing eyes as the day drifted lazily into dream-time.

'What'll we call him?' he murmured, and Molly hugged him closer.

'How about Lionel Two?' she suggested, and Jackson laughed.

'Great. Here we have the beginning of a frog dynasty called Lionel.'

'And Mr Baird…' It was all Sam could do to speak. His lids were closing regardless, but there was still urgency. 'You will teach me to swim tomorrow?'

'I will teach you to swim tomorrow,' Jackson told him, and stooped to place a hand on the little boy's face. Gently he closed his eyes. 'Now, go to sleep, young man. Your aunt and I will clean up here and then carry you up to your bed.'

But Sam was no longer listening. Sam was asleep already.

It was just plain magic and there was no disputing it.

'In Scotland they called this the gloaming,' Molly said softly, watching the sleeping child beside her. She was sleepy herself—warm and tired and happy as she hadn't been warm and tired and happy for years.

'The gloaming?' Jackson paused from packing to look a question.

'It's the magic time between the ending of the day's work and the time for rest,' she told him. 'It's when the world pauses for breath. And waits. It doesn't know what it's waiting for, but anything can happen in the gloaming. It's full of promise for tomorrow and tomorrow after that.'

She was talking nonsense, she thought, her eyes resting on the sleeping Sam. He was curled against her on the rug, his dark lashes fluttering down under his too heavy glasses and his hand clutching a fistful of seashells. She loved this little boy so much...

The gloaming—this magic time of day—was a time of healing for Sam.

And for herself?

Definitely for herself.

She looked up and found Jackson watching her, and the expression in his eyes took her breath away.

'We'd best get back to the house,' she murmured, but the expression on his face made Molly falter. He was looking at her as if he couldn't believe what he was seeing.

But finally he found his voice. He knelt, and his hand came out to touch Sam's hair. 'Poor little tyke. It's so damned unfair—that he's lost so much.'

His sympathy touched her as nothing else could. 'It is.' She managed a smile. 'But he's had a wonderful day—thanks to you.'

'And thanks to you. He's safe now. His time of desperate sadness is past. He'll move on.'

'How do you know?'

'I watched him tonight. He was letting go. Trusting. Placing bets on the world again and finding it not too bad a place after all.'

'I hope so.'

'I'm sure of it.' And, as if propelled by forces out of his control, he put out a hand and traced her cheekbone, from her eyelids to the corner of her chin, where a tiny dimple peeped.

She didn't move. She sat still as stone, willing it to happen.

It was the gloaming. The magic time. What happened now wouldn't be taken forward. What happened now was for now.

'Molly…'

She looked wonderingly into his face, her eyes a question.

'Mmm?'

He didn't know what to say, and when he found something it was inadequate. Far too inadequate. 'You're beautiful.'

She grinned. 'Well, I guess that's quite a compliment, coming from you.'

'What's that supposed to mean?'

'I mean you've been photographed with some of the world's loveliest women.'

'You're just as lovely.'

'Yes?' She managed to keep smiling, but heaven knew it was hard. Somehow she forced a joke. 'Gregor wouldn't agree. There's sand between my toes, Mr Baird. *Sand!*'

He chuckled, but he didn't move. He stayed kneeling before her, taking in the sight of her, her smile, the way the child nestled in beside her.

Hell, he wanted to be part of this, he thought suddenly. Molly was faced with such a burden. He could help.

'Do you need anything?' he asked, and Molly frowned.

'What do you mean?'

'I mean…' He hesitated. Maybe it was the wrong thing to say, but it needed to be said. 'I mean financially.'

A flicker of anger built from within. This was such a wondrous time—how dared he spoil it by talking about money? She shook her head, aware that the magic was fading. 'No. Thank you very much, but you've helped enough. You've given us today, and you're giving Sam tomorrow.' She hesitated. 'You do intend to keep your promise to teach him to swim?'

'I'll keep my promise.'

'Well, there you go.' She smiled. 'That's enough. So thank you.'

'But after that? You'll let me help?'

'You're going overseas,' she reminded him. 'You're not much help there.'

'But financially I could help.'

Again the anger. Was he obtuse? 'I told you, I don't need money.'

'Well, what do you need?'

The man was totally insensitive. What did she need? What a question—when more and more she was starting to think what she needed was kneeling right in front of her.

But he couldn't know that. He couldn't see how vulnerable she really was.

'I need friends,' she muttered, and then she softened. 'I can't be more specific than that, but that's what I do need—and Sam needs friends, too. People who'll be there for us.' She gave him a rueful smile. 'Not people who jet around the world and are only in Australia one month in twelve. If that.'

Friends. He could do friends. Even if it was only for a month... 'Then maybe I could see you again? When I'm in the country?'

'Sam would like that.' She met his eyes and her expression was a challenge. 'But we won't count on it. You promised Sam you'd take him swimming and it's important—more important than you know—that you keep that promise. And you said you'd bring his frogs back here, and that's important, too. But apart from that...please don't make promises you can't keep, Mr Baird.'

'Jackson,' he growled, and she nodded.

'Okay, Jackson. But, please—'

'Leave you alone? Is that what you're asking?'

'I don't know.' But suddenly she did know. This man had the capacity to tilt her world, and the last six months had seen her world tilted quite enough. So there was only one way to answer him. 'Yes.'

They stared at each other for a long, long minute.

She wasn't just asking for Sam, Jackson thought. She was asking for herself. Don't offer what you can't follow though with. Don't play with us. Don't break our hearts.

Damn.

And she was looking at him as if he had the capacity to do just that. It unmanned him. It made him want to make all sorts of rash promises. Promises she knew already that he couldn't keep.

But still she watched him. The sun had slipped below the horizon and the moon wasn't yet up. The soft, rose-coloured hues of the horizon were playing over the beach, shifting the colour of the sand, reflecting in the enormity of Molly's eyes. She was so beautiful.

He couldn't help himself.

Just once, he thought, and he leant and took her face in his hands. And kissed her.

Well, why not? The child was deeply asleep on the rug beside them. There was no-one but this man and this woman. And what harm was there in a kiss?

None, but if the kiss was a seal on a promise…

And that was what it felt like. It was a promise half made and now met head-on. Two halves of a whole, meeting and merging and becoming their rightful one.

This was their second kiss. The first had been a kiss of triumph—of warmth and laughter and joy. This took it further. This was no light kiss between a man and a woman with common cause for joy. This was a kiss that took one man and joined him to one woman for ever.

For the heat that flooded through them was unimagined—a heat that neither had experienced before. It felt so right. So much a part of them. Because it was what both had been searching for for life, but neither had known until this moment.

The kiss deepened and deepened again. They were kneeling on the sand, the sleeping child beside them. The waves were washing in and out, unnoticed but forming a glorious backdrop for their passion. The moon was just above the horizon, setting its silver ribbon of light across the surf—aimed just at them.

As a blessing...

His hands held her close, exploring her body, feeling the softness and the yielding wonder of her. His mouth tasted her, savoured her, gloried in her...

And for Molly, after that first moment of shock as his mouth met hers, she knew that this was where she wanted to be for the rest of her life. That whatever this man asked of her she was prepared to give. Because, in a sense, she'd given already. She'd given her heart.

He was so large and so male. The feel of his fingers in her hair sent heat surging right through her body. She gloried in him. Her tongue tasted him, needed him, took him, and when his hands slipped down the soft cotton of her bra and caressed the soft curves of her breasts it was as much as she could do not to groan with pleasure.

Dear heaven... Oh, love...

Her fingers moved to slip inside his shirt so she could feel the nakedness of his chest, feel his nipples, feel the muscles across his chest and the way his whole body was taut with desire. Taut with desire for her.

Oh, love...

This couldn't last. She knew it couldn't. Jackson Baird was right out of her league. But for now he was kissing her and she wanted nothing more. All she wanted was that this wonder flooding through them both should be allowed to run its own sweet course—to take them where it willed within the kiss itself.

Neither could break the moment.

Molly's face was in Jackson's hands again, and her sweetness was threatening to engulf him. Her joy, her love of life, her laughter—damn, even her efficiency. All of her. All of her was in this kiss, and he'd never felt anything so wonderful in his life.

Her body was pliant in his hands. Her sweetness was in his heart. She was a world away from anyone he'd ever met.

She was Molly...

He wanted her so badly. He felt his body stiffen with desire and gave an almost audible groan. Some things weren't possible. Not here. Not now. Even if he'd brought precautions, there was the child to consider.

As if on cue Sam stirred between them and sighed in his sleep. Not much, but enough. It was enough to break the link—to let reality glimmer in.

And with reality came confusion. They were left staring at each other in the waxing moonlight, neither knowing where to take this. Neither understanding what had happened. Only knowing that it had happened and life itself had somehow been transformed.

The silence lasted into the stillness as the moon rose over the clouds and burst forth in all its glory. The glimmer of silver became a shaft of glorious, shimmering wonder—they were on a knife-edge and it could go either way.

But in the end sense won. Of course sense won. When had it not?

'I'm...I'm sorry,' Jackson murmured into the stillness, and he somehow broke away to stand apart from her. It had needed only that for Molly to haul herself together—to banish the confusion she was feeling and replace the sensation with anger. Sorry!

'You hardly seduced me,' she muttered, and pulled backwards, gathering Sam into her arms as though the sleeping child was a shield. 'It was one kiss—and I kissed you right back.'

One kiss does not a relationship make, her tone said, and Jackson took a deep breath and thought, She's right. There were so many other factors at play here. This was not sensible. It was not even possible!

His future was mapped out. Sensible and settled. Just him and his half-sister against the world...

'Give me Sam.' He stooped and lifted the child from her, using the movement to pull himself together. Then he stood cradling the little boy to him and looking down at Molly as she hauled their picnic stuff together. She wasn't looking at him.

Maybe she couldn't.

'Time to go home?' he said softly, and she shoved the last things in the picnic hamper and rose. She was angry, but it was impossible for him to tell if she was angry with him or with herself.

'Yes,' she said briefly. 'It's time to go home.'

'It's been a wonderful night.'

'Apart from the past few moments,' she muttered. 'And they were just plain stupid!'


Just plain stupid?

Jackson lay awake into the night and thought about those words. Just plain stupid.

She was right, he thought. It was stupid. Because they were worlds apart.

Why?

The question hammered him in the dark. Why was it so impossible?

Because she didn't understand.

Understand what?

Understand him.

Hell, he should have had more sense than to ever let a relationship get this far, he told himself savagely in the dark.

Unbidden, a vision of his parents came into his mind—his parents as he remembered them best. He'd been about four at the time, and it was the same sort of ugliness that had dogged him all through his childhood. There'd never been any doubt that his parents loved each other, but they'd seemed intent on destroying each other from the time he could first remember.

So their relationship had been a series of tumultuous merges. They'd come together with mutual need and their love would hold them for maybe a day. Maybe not even for that long. Then the tempers would flare again, with Jackson caught in the middle.

He'd been used as a tool. A weapon.

'You love me most, don't you Jackson?' his mother would demand of him, and his father would grasp his hand and try and drag him away.

'The boy wants to be with me.'

The boy hadn't wanted to be anywhere, and the boy who'd become a man was just the same. If that was love he wanted no part of it.

You don't recover from that sort of damage, Jackson thought bleakly. How could he ever admit to himself that he could love like that? It wasn't a wonderful emotion you could sink into. It left you exposed to pain and then more pain after that. And then there'd been Diane, and that had hurt still more.

So now he was solitary, and he liked it that way. His father had walked out for the final time when he was ten years old and his mother had punished him the best—or the worst—way she could think of. She'd had an affair that had resulted in Cara—and when that hadn't been enough for her she'd driven herself furiously into a tree. Because of love…

Love could go take a hike, he told himself into the night. He'd take care of Cara and no one else. He wanted no emotional dependence. Ever.

'Mr Baird is nice,' Sam murmured sleepily to Molly as she tucked him into bed. His arms came up to claim her for a goodnight kiss. Such a gesture was unusual, to say the least, and Molly sat down on the bed and hugged him back.

'Yes, Sam. He is nice.'

'He kissed you.'

So Sam hadn't been soundly asleep. There was no sense in denying it. 'He did.'

And Sam was off and running. 'Do you think he might like us enough to marry you?'

'Hey.' She laughed, but her laugh was decidedly hollow. 'We've only known the man since yesterday.'

'But he *is* nice.'

'He's very nice. But the man's a millionaire, Sam. The likes of him don't look at the likes of us.'

'Why not?'

'He'll marry someone of his own class.'

'That's silly.' He was drifting into sleep but refusing to be shifted from his lovely fantasy. 'And what's class?'

'It's like the case of Cinderella and the Prince,' she told

him, rumpling his hair and removing his glasses to lay them on the bedside table. 'The way I see it, it would have been pretty uncomfortable to be Cinderella.'

'Why?'

'Because she'd have had to say thank you for the rest of her life and she wouldn't have liked it.'

'Maybe Cinderella could have got a job, like lots of married ladies do. Like you.' He giggled. 'Cinderella could have sold palaces for a living.'

She grinned at the image. 'Oh, sure. And she'd sell glass slippers on the side. You're letting your commercial ventures run away with you, kiddo.' She kissed him soundly. 'Now—sleep, young man.'

'But what about you and Mr Baird?'

'You know, there's about as much chance of me kissing your frog, Lionel, and having him turn into a handsome prince as there is of me kissing Jackson Baird and having him propose marriage.'

Sam liked that. He chuckled sleepily and turned towards his frog box.

'Lionel might like it if you kissed him.'

'And after Mr Gray went to all that trouble to find a Mrs Lionel for him!' Molly rose and grinned. 'Mrs Lionel might have something to say to any frog-kissing I might like to do.'

'You're funny.'

'No.' The smile died from her eyes as she stooped to tuck his covers closer. 'Just sensible. Someone has to be.'

'Miss Copeland?'

After a sleepless night Molly rose early to catch the elderly lady at home. From what she knew of old ladies she'd be more likely to find her alert at breakfast than at midnight, and frankly she hadn't had herself enough in control to phone last night.

She was right in her guesswork. Hannah Copeland answered on the first ring and sounded wide awake. 'Yes, dear. I was hoping you'd call.' Molly had talked to her briefly on Friday night, so the elderly landowner knew what to expect. 'Does he like my farm?'

'He wants to buy.'

'Oh, I am pleased. That's very nice, dear. Is three million too much?'

'It's a very reasonable price. To be honest, you could ask more. If you were willing to subdivide...'

'No, dear, I do not want to subdivide.'

'It's just the place is really worth much more. Are you sure you want to sell?'

'To the right buyer—yes, I am.'

'And you think Jackson Baird is the right buyer?'

There was a pause on the other end of the line, as if the lady was considering how much it was wise to tell. Finally she decided to be frank. 'My mother was a friend of Jackson Baird's grandmother,' she told her. 'She was so worried about Jackson. Has he turned out well, dear?'

Molly blinked. 'I...yes. I guess you could say he's turned out very well.'

'He's not married?'

'Um...no.'

'I didn't expect he would be after those awful parents.' She paused as Molly waited. 'But my mother and his grandmother worried so much about him, and I know they'd approve of me doing this.'

'Miss Copeland, I don't think Jackson Baird needs any favours,' Molly said bluntly. 'The man's extremely wealthy.' She hesitated, but the silence on the end of the line told her to move on. So she did. 'You did say on Friday that if he was interested there were a couple of stipulations you'd make?'

'Yes.'

'The Grays being one of them?'

'You guessed?' Her pleasure sounded down the line. 'Of course. I'd never want Gregor or Doreen to have to move.'

'I'm sure Jackson will agree to that.'

'And I trust you. You have a lovely voice. Mrs Gray says you have a little boy?'

'Doreen rang you?'

'Yesterday.'

'You don't mind that I brought Sam?'

'Of course I don't mind, dear. The place needs children. I'd rather hoped that despite his parents' example Mr Baird might have a wife himself. Do you think he's the marrying kind?'

Whew. Molly shook her head at that one. 'I can hardly ask him,' she said frankly. 'Don't tell me you want to make that a condition of sale?'

'No.' But she sounded wistful. 'I'm no matchmaker. But I do want my farm to go to someone who'll love it as I have.' There was a pause, then, 'I'd like to meet Jackson. In person.'

'I'm sure we can arrange that.'

'And I want to meet you. Will you bring him to lunch with me on Monday?'

'I think my boss—'

'No. You.'

Molly thought that through. Fine. If that was what it took to get a sale... 'I'll check with Jackson now. Can I bring the contract to lunch?'

'Bring whatever you want.' The old lady's smile sounded down the phone. 'But don't book anything else for the afternoon. I like long lunches.'

\* \* \*

Molly had a very long shower and when she met Jackson over the breakfast table she was formality itself.

'Good morning. How did you sleep?'

He'd decided on formality as well, but now it was pushed on him he didn't like it very much. Two could play at this game.

'Fine, thank you. And you?'

'Like a top,' she lied.

'Where's Sam?'

'He ate at dawn with Mr Gray,' she told him. 'It seems they had an assignation. The frog croaking just before sunrise is truly wonderful. Gregor's told him that there are ten different species to be listened to.'

'Fantastic.'

'It is fantastic.' She was prattling like a fool, and serving herself far too much from the feast filling the kitchen table. 'I've rung Miss Copeland.'

'My, you have been busy.'

'It's my job to be busy.'

'Of course.'

'Don't you want to hear what she had to say?' She poured a glass of orange juice so fast she spilled it. Oh, for heaven's sake, she was acting like a schoolgirl.

'I do want to hear what she has to say.' He sank courteously into a chair and waited for her to recover.

'She says she'll sell—as long as you keep Doreen and Gregor on and you meet her for lunch on Monday and you turn out to be a nice person.'

'A *nice* person?' He raised a quizzical eyebrow.

'She didn't elaborate.' She shrugged. 'It seems money itself isn't the aim of the exercise. I have a feeling if she doesn't like you—or even if she doesn't like me—then she'll pull out of the sale. So it's up to the pair of us to

define nice.' She already had. She was staring at her plate—
at anything rather than him.

But he was looking straight at her, considering. 'You
know, it *is* underpriced.'

'That's hardly the line of an eager buyer.' She concentrated again on her orange juice—concentrated really, really
hard. She didn't want this man to be nice, she thought. She
wanted the ruthless businessman she'd heard of. Ruthless
she could cope with. For some reason nice made her want
to weep.

Then Sam yelled from outside the window and stomped
in to find them. Molly was almost glad of the interruption.

'We counted eleven different frog calls! Mr Gray says
he's hard pushed to tell the difference, but he's got a re-
cording that'll tell us in the library. He says it's time for
breakfast and then we can go swimming. Can we go swimming, Mr Baird?'

Jackson's eyes met Molly's and he smiled—she was way
out of her depth all over again, and she stayed out of her
depth all day.


And it was some day—a day full of Jackson. She watched
him swim with her small nephew. She watched him pa-
tiently take Sam step by step through the early stages of
swimming as if he had all the time in the world and this
was the most important thing he could do with his time.

She watched him laugh with triumph as Sam conquered
floating, and she watched his eyes swing up the beach to
find her. The message they held was pure, unadulterated
delight. He could as well have been a child himself.

Where was the ruthless businessman now?

She watched him towel Sam dry and tow the sleepy little
boy back to the farmhouse. And she watched him devour

another of Doreen's enormous meals and compliment her, then share a joke with Gregor and...

And twist each and every one of them round his little finger, she thought. The man's charm had them all in thrall.

There was a side to Jackson that she hadn't seen, she thought desperately. There must be. He hadn't gained his fearsome reputation for nothing. So beware...

But her heart wasn't being the least fearful. Her heart wasn't being the least bit sensible.

Her heart was falling head over heels in love with Jackson Baird.

# CHAPTER SEVEN

'FRANCIS?'

'Mr Baird.' Roger Francis answered on the first ring and his tension was palpable. 'What's the decision?'

'No decision yet. The property is just what I've been looking for but I'm required to meet the owner. It seems the old lady's only selling if she approves of me *and* if she approves of the selling agent. She's set up a lunch for us both tomorrow.'

'And if things don't go well?'

'Then I'll be back looking at the Blue Mountain property again. And it may well happen. As I said, she seems just as interested in her saleswoman as she is in me. She sounds a real eccentric—but then at her age and with her degree of wealth I guess it's her prerogative.'

'Sure.' But Roger didn't sound sure. He sounded tense as hell.

Well, it was late on Sunday night, Jackson thought. Maybe he'd interrupted something important. But the man was on his payroll; he was paid to be on call at all hours and he hardly ever earned his keep. And there was something Jackson wanted him to do.

'You want me to check the titles?'

'Um…no.'

'Then what…?'

'I want you to check the saleswoman.'

'Pardon?'

'Molly Farr.' Jackson hesitated, knowing he was stepping over the line of reasonable business practice. But he

108

guessed she was in financial trouble and he wanted to know how badly.

'I want a bit of background briefing,' he told him. 'In a hurry.'

'Molly?'

'Michael!'

'Molly, love...'

What on earth was he on about? Molly had barely walked in the door before the phone had started to ring, and when she'd recognised her ex-fiancé's voice she'd come close to dropping the receiver. 'I can't believe I'm hearing this. *What did you call me?*'

'Molly, we need to talk. Something's come up.'

There was only one answer to that. 'Talk to whoever you like. Just don't talk to me.'

Slam.

'Cara?'

'Jackson, love, I wasn't expecting another call so soon...'

'Cara, I need to tell you about this property. It's fantastic. If we can get it then I think it's just what we've been looking for.'

'That's marvellous.' She hesitated. 'Is anything wrong?'

'What should be wrong?'

'I don't know. You sound sort of absent.'

'I am in Australia.'

'That must be it.'

'Are you willing to come and see it—before I sign on the dotted line?'

Another hesitation. 'Darling, I am busy. And Australia's so far.'

He let his irritation show through at that. 'Well, I'm

busy, too. But this is for long term, Cara. If you can't put in a bit of effort…'

'Okay. Okay. I'll make time. If it's important.'

'It is.'

'Roger? It's Michael.'

'Mmm?'

'It's not going to work. She won't have a bar of me.'

# CHAPTER EIGHT

MICHAEL'S odd phone call from out of the blue had done little to settle her mood.

It was strange, Molly thought. Until Friday she'd thought of Michael a dozen times a day. She'd been desperate for him to explain the unexplainable. Now it was as if he had simply ceased to exist. And it wasn't Michael who was doing the unsettling.

Jackson had seen them into a taxi at the airport. 'Until tomorrow,' he'd told her, and he'd placed a finger on her lips as a farewell gesture. 'Sleep well.'

The pressure of his touch had stayed with her as she'd slammed the phone down on Michael. It had been with her as she'd put Sam to bed. It was with her still, and when her doorbell pealed she drifted towards it as if she was almost floating. This night seemed so magical anything could happen.

But it wasn't Jackson. Of course it wasn't Jackson. Angela was on her doorstep, as she'd promised she would be—an Angela with crimson spots burning on her cheeks, her eyes bright with laughter and mock indignation.

'Will you look at this?' she demanded the minute Molly opened the door. She stalked inside and held up a newspaper. 'Oh, and I had such wonderful plans.'

'I... What?' Molly stood back to let her friend stalk past. Angela, it seemed, was in the mood for stalking.

'The man's not what he seems. He got all my hopes up.

Here I was, planning weddings and honeymoons and limousines and mansions—and look! The man's spoken for.'

Molly thought that through, but she was confused. 'Um… Guy's spoken for?' It seemed crazy.

'As if.' Angela glowered, and then managed a rueful smile. 'Not that it wouldn't be a very good thing if Guy found Another. That man! You know what he wore to his Roaring Twenties party? A dinner suit! A dinner suit, I ask you. When I went to so much trouble and the man wouldn't even wear white shoes. And now this.'

'Now what?' Angela was waving her newspaper like a flag and Molly couldn't see a thing. 'If you're not planning yours, whose wedding were you planning?'

'Yours, of course. With Jackson Baird.' Angela moaned. 'And now he has some woman called Cara…'

Silence.

She shouldn't mind, Molly thought abstractedly, and in a way she didn't. She felt disassociated. Adrift. As if she was someone else. As if this conversation had nothing to do with her.

'Can I see?' she said at last, and Angela cast her an odd glance. Angela's face was still flushed with mock indignation, but it was fading and she was starting to watch Molly carefully. Her friend's reaction wasn't what she'd expected. This was meant to be a joke—but there was no laughter here.

This was suddenly serious.

'Page three.'

And Molly read.

  Rumour has it that Jackson Baird is spending the weekend assessing one of New South Wales' foremost pastoral properties, with the intention of purchasing it as his base in Australia. Baird, known until now for inhabiting expensive penthouses, is in the market for a rural property to share with Cara Lyons, international model and renowned horsewoman. More news as it comes to hand. Watch this space.

'The fink,' Angela said, but her fire had died. She was watching Molly very cautiously indeed.

'There's no reason why he's a fink. The man has a perfect right to share his property with whoever he likes.'

'But not to tell us!'

'It's hardly in the sales contract. It's none of our business.'

'No. But...' Angela's eyes narrowed. 'You look... different. Did you get close to the man?'

'Uh...yes.'

Angela's bubble of laughter had disappeared completely. 'Did he kiss you?'

Molly fumbled with the buttons of her bathrobe. 'He might have.' Then at Angela's indignant gasp she managed a smile. 'Well, why not? I'd imagine he's kissed thousands of women.'

'And a little thing like another woman shouldn't stand in his way?'

'I guess not.' But it hurt. It hurt far more than she thought possible.

'You're nuts.'

'I'm a businesswoman,' Molly managed. 'For heaven's sake, I don't know what you're carrying on about. Anything between us is out of the question.'

'Yet still he kissed you.' Angela took a deep breath. 'Molly, I'd just die to be kissed by a hunk like that.'

'I'm almost sure you wouldn't.'

'And I'm sure I would.'

The firmness of Angela's tone was startling, and Molly

steadied. Okay, she had problems, but there was more to this than met the eye. And concentrating on Angela meant that she could stop concentrating on Jackson. She steered her friend into a lounge chair. 'Problems with Guy, huh?'

'Nothing that a little affair with Jackson Baird couldn't sort out,' Angela said bitterly—and then, almost longingly, 'Did you kiss him back?'

'It's none of your business.'

'But wouldn't it be wonderful…' She sighed again, and decided to change tack. 'You made the sale?'

'I made the sale.'

'Does Trevor know?'

'I rang him before we left Birraginbil.'

'He'll be over the moon. But…' Angela was clearly not thinking about Trevor's commission. 'Are you seeing him again?'

'Who, Trevor?'

'You know very well who I mean.'

'Tomorrow. For lunch.'

'Oh, Moll…'

'With the property owner. And, according to this, maybe even with someone called Cara.' Molly looked at Cara's photograph under the newsprint and thought, Wow! And then, How could I ever compete with someone like this?

She couldn't. It was as simple as that.

But Angela was still on track. 'Oh.' A sigh of disappointment, but then, 'Well, that's something. You can work on it from there.'

'And he's leaving for the States on Tuesday—that's the day after tomorrow.'

'So work fast.'

'Will you cut it out?'

'But you kissed him.'

'I don't think even marriage vows will stop Jackson kissing women,' Molly snapped. 'The man's seriously…'

'Seriously?'

'Seriously gorgeous.' There. She'd said it. She plonked herself down on the chair opposite Angela and spread her hands in a plea.

'Help,' she said.

'Help?'

'Help. I'm in trouble.'

'Trouble,' Angela said cautiously. 'What sort of trouble?'

'I've been stupid.'

'Like?'

'Like I think I've fallen head over heels in love,' she told her friend bluntly. She had to tell someone or she'd go mad. Or maybe she was mad anyway. 'I know. I'm nuts. I'm stark staring nuts,' she said. 'And I have as much chance of attracting the man as flying, but there it is.'

'Oh, Molly.'

'And he's not even sensible, like your Guy is. He's way out of my league. He's—'

'You know, sensible is not all that terrific,' Angela interrupted flatly. 'I think unsensible has a whole heap going for it.'

'Not when he's committed to someone else.'

'We don't know how committed.'

'They're buying a farm together.'

'There is that.'

'Got any ideas?'

'I'm thinking.' Angela shook her head in bewilderment. 'What with your playboy Jackson and my boring Guy, I'm thinking so hard I'm threatening to burst. Why don't they teach us this stuff in property sales school? How to avoid accountants and ensnare rich clients.'

'Ensnare rich clients with no strings attached. It's not possible.'

'We could try.' She cast Molly a helpless glance. '*You* could try. Tomorrow.'

'Yeah, right. So tomorrow I see him and I know full well he's committed to another woman. You think I should sweep him off his feet?'

'He can't be all that committed if he's kissing you.' But Angela didn't sound convinced.

'Attached enough to be buying a farm for them to share. And don't forget I'm not exactly footloose and fancy-free myself. I'm encumbered with one small boy.'

'Yet you're in love?'

There was only one answer to that. 'Yes. I'm in love.'

'Boy, you're in deeper trouble than I am. Or just as much.' Angela glared down at her diamond and suddenly tugged it from her finger, put it on the coffee table and regarded it with loathing. 'There. There's two of us in trouble now. Talk about sisterhood. But if you're unhappy then I'm unhappy. Guy's the most boring man on earth and I'm not putting that ring back on 'til he does something outrageous.'

'Like what?'

'Like…like kissing me like he really means it. Like wearing braces that don't match his tie. Like not tying his shoelaces with the knots his grandmother taught him, or wearing black shoes with brown trousers. Or not putting every penny he earns into sensible investments or trading in his boring car for a honeymoon in the Bahamas. I don't know. *Anything!* Unless it's predictable.'

'It's not going to happen,' Molly told her, and they sat and stared at each other in increasing misery.

'What we need here is something for really desperate people,' Angela said at last, coming to a decision because someone had to. She rose and tossed her keys onto the sideboard. 'I'm off to the supermarket and I'm walking, because just thinking about what I'm going to buy will put me over the legal alcohol limit.'

'What are you going to buy?'

'Irish cream, Tia Maria ice cream and an industrial sized packet of Tim Tams,' her friend told her. 'That should fix all the men in our lives. Properly.'

Molly opened one eye and shut it again. Firmly. Mistake, she thought. Big mistake. On a scale of one to ten, it fell off the counter.

'Molly?'

It was Sam. He was bending over her, lifting an eyelid. 'Are you in there?'

'No.' She groaned and he chuckled.

'Yes, you are. Angela was asleep in the lounge room. She told me she wasn't in there either, but she is really. And you haven't washed your dishes. There's empty ice cream tubs, which I don't think is fair because I didn't eat any, but you haven't finished all the Tim Tams so I ate seven for breakfast.' He burped a very satisfactory small boy burp and grinned. 'And now we're going to be late.'

Oh, help. Molly lifted one eyelid a fraction of an inch and checked the time. And yelped. Late! She'd be lucky to be on time for the afternoon shift. And Sam should be at school. What sort of a responsible guardian was she, anyway?

But this *was* the first time he'd been late in the six months she'd been taking care of him. Maybe it wasn't a hanging offence. She groaned and eyed her nephew with caution.

'Sam, do you suppose you could work really, really hard

and still be a brain surgeon if I declare this morning a holiday?'

Sam considered, his grin growing broader. Where had this grin come from? Molly thought, shaken out of her bleariness by its intensity. On Friday it had been as if his face would crack if he smiled. Now the grins were coming fast and furious.

'Why is it a holiday?' he asked, and Molly sought for inspiration.

'It's National Frog Day,' she said promptly, and his lovely giggle filled her room.

'You are silly.'

'Yeah, and I'm also risking being sacked. Though I have just made the world's biggest sale.' She sat up and rubbed her eyes. 'Sorry, pet. Have you been awake for long?'

'Mr Baird woke me up.'

'Mr *Baird?*'

'The doorbell went and I opened it,' he told her. 'He's here and he's brought a froghouse. In bits. We have to build it. It's in the lounge room. Angela was there, but when I said come in to Mr Baird she went, "Yikes!" and she's now in my bedroom, in my bed, with the bedcovers drawn up over her head. Do you think Mr Baird will give me another swimming lesson?'

'I doubt it.' The temptation to join Angela was almost overwhelming. 'Um…is Mr Baird still here?'

'Of course he is. With his present. The froghouse legs are in bits on the lounge room floor and I've been helping him read the instructions. We want to know where to put it, 'cos Mr Baird says he's blowed if he's moving it after it's assembled. So he said I'd better wake you up, hangover or not.' He peered closely at his dishevelled aunt. 'That's what he said. *Have* you got a hangover?'

'No. Yes!' Molly was staring at her nephew as if he'd grown horns. 'He's out there now?'

'Yes.'

'Tell him to go away.'

'Tell him yourself.' The voice was deep and growly and wonderfully familiar—and it made Molly jump a foot. She swivelled to find Jackson standing in the doorway, and by his unholy grin she knew he was enjoying himself very much indeed. 'But why you'd want to I don't know.'

'What are you doing here?'

'That's not a nice way to greet a guest. Especially a guest who's brought a gift.'

'What gift?'

'I told you. He's brought us a froghouse,' Sam explained, as if she was being deliberately obtuse. 'It's the hugest fishpond, but we're not filling it all with water. It's set up so there's ponds and a waterfall and rocks for them to lie on. But we can't get the legs together. Guy says the book of instructions reads like we're building the Taj Mahal.'

*'Guy?'* What on earth was Angela's fiancé doing here?

'Hi,' Guy said over Jackson's shoulder, and Molly's jaw dropped somewhere round her waist.

'Guy...'

'That's me.' The man managed a smile, but only just.

'Does Angela know you're here?' She was practically squeaking.

'Yes, but she's locked the bedroom door,' he told her, and he sounded bewildered. 'She was mad at me because I wouldn't wear white shoes. White shoes, for heaven's sake. Then, when I started talking about our wedding and said we needed to have my sisters as bridesmaids, and maybe it was time we found a nice house in the suburbs, she started burbling about elopements and purple warehouses and I couldn't make head nor tail of it. She walked

out on me. I've been looking for her all weekend and Sam
says she's here but she won't talk to me. Molly, why is her
engagement ring on the coffee table rather than on her finger?'

It was too much for Molly. 'I don't know. Go away. The
lot of you.' She was clutching her sheet and thinking her
bathrobe was too far away to reach...

'We had a big night, then, did we?' Jackson asked. He
was leaning against the doorjamb, his arms crossed over
his chest in a pose that was starting to seem dangerously
familiar. He sounded full of commiseration, but his wide
smile was filled with laughter.

'You especially,' she flashed at him. 'Get out of my bedroom. Now!'

'She doesn't want us.' Jackson's big hand dropped to
Sam's shoulder in a gesture so familiar it had Molly's heart
doing backflips. 'Sam, boy, we're being rejected.'

'At least she hasn't taken your ring off,' Guy told him,
as lugubrious as a bloodhound on a bad day, and Jackson
nodded.

'There is that. I guess I should be grateful for small mer-
cies. Molly, where do you want us to put your froghouse?'

'I don't *want* a froghouse!' Molly practically yelled.

'Molly!' Sam said, shocked.

'Of course you want a froghouse,' Jackson told her. 'You
can't keep using the bathroom floor. Someone's going to
step on one. Or...' His eyes glinted with laughter. 'They
might hop down the toilet. Have you thought of that?'

Oh, for heaven's sake!

'It'd be an environmental nightmare if they reached the
sewerage system.'

If only he'd stop laughing. She gritted her teeth. In fact
she gritted every bone in her body and refused to respond
to that gorgeous, wicked laughter. 'Go away or I'll scream.'

'Why will you scream?' Sam asked, interested, and Molly almost groaned. How on earth was she going to get out of this one?

But Jackson relented. Laughing, he took Sam's hand—and there went Molly's insides again in their familiar lurch—and drew him out of the room. He propelled Guy with him.

'We men will be out in the living room when you're up to receiving visitors,' he told her, still laughing. 'Meanwhile, Sam—unless you'd like to see your aunty Molly have an apoplexy, which I admit is a very interesting prospect but maybe risky for all concerned—we'd better vamoose.'

'Vamoose?'

'Leave your aunty Molly to recover.'


'Angie?'

No answer.

'Angela!' Molly had hauled on a wrap and pulled a comb through her curls—she was now almost respectable—but she wanted support if she was to go into *that* living room. Supper last night had been Angela's idea, so Angela could help her face the consequences.

'Angie!' The two bedrooms were off a central passage leading to the living room. As she tried Angela's door Molly was acutely aware of the silence, and she just knew everyone was listening. She twiddled the doorknob and found it locked.

'Come on out. I refuse to face this lot by myself.'

Nothing.

'I'll fix you.' Angela was sleeping—sleeping—ha!—in Sam's room, and the door had a child lock on it. That was, it could be locked, but in an emergency Molly could slip a nail file or a pair of scissors into the tiny slot and...

And the door opened first go.

But inside there was no Angela. There was only an empty bed and a wide open window with drapes blowing outward. With a sinking heart Molly peered out—in time to see her friend hiking off down the street as fast as her legs could carry her. She was wearing her mini-skirt of the night before, buttoning her blouse as she went and carrying her stilettos under one arm.

'Don't do this to me!' she yelled to Angie's retreating back, but just then a taxi pulled up and Angela clambered in with the speed of light. There was a wave of a frantic hand and the taxi headed out of sight.

Her friend had left her without a backward glance.

'Oh, Angela, you fink…'

And then she turned and faced the living room door.

Help.

Sink or swim. There was no choice. She went to face the music. Alone.


It was far easier to concentrate on Guy than it was to even think about Jackson. Jackson and Sam were surrounded by construction plans, but Guy was standing by the coffee table, staring down at the ring as if it meant the end of the world as he knew it.

'Hell.' He lifted the ring and stared down at it, then peered down the passage. 'Is Angie still there?'

Molly shook her head. 'She's gone.'

Guy sighed, his big shoulders slumping. He might be a very boring accountant, Molly thought, but right at this minute she felt sorry for him. He stood in his blue pinstripe suit with matching waistcoat, looking the very epitome of a successful accountant—and he looked as if he'd lost the world.

'Maybe you should go after her,' she suggested.

'She won't let me into her apartment. I was practically sure she was home, but she hasn't been answering her door all weekend.'

Molly thought that through and nodded, but an idea was forming. 'You know, Guy, you may well have an advantage.' She motioned to the keys on the sideboard. 'Those are Angie's keys.'

Guy stared. 'Her keys?'

'They're her car keys and her apartment keys. She left here with nothing.' She managed a smile. 'So she's in trouble. Her handbag's also still here, and she's caught a taxi. She won't have the money to pay and she won't be able to get into her apartment. Guy, if you were intent on doing a spot of rescuing, now's the time to do it.'

Guy thought this through, his accountant's mind adding it all up. But it didn't compute. Behind him Jackson had ceased reading plans and was watching. Waiting… 'I don't understand.'

She smiled at him. 'Guy, do you need to understand to be a hero?'

Silence. Finally he lifted the engagement ring and squared his shoulders—then glanced to the construction site. 'If you can do without me…?'

'We'll manage without you,' Jackson said magnanimously. He cast Molly a curious look. 'No keys and no money. Angie's needs sound a lot more dire than ours.'

'And Guy?' Molly said gently, and he paused, hand on the doorknob.

'Yes?'

'If you want my advice you'd think about the desirability of elopement, you'd cut back on bridesmaids, you'd buy yourself a pair of white shoes and you'd stop on the way and buy out a florist.'

He thought that through. 'You mean buy her a bunch of flowers?'

The man was thick as Sam's frogs. 'No, Guy, I do not mean a bunch. What Angela needs is a statement. You need to buy a carload of flowers. Or a truckload, for that matter.'

'What…? Why…?'

She sighed. 'Guy, she's left her jacket here and it's cold. She'll be sitting on the landing, feeling bereft and sorry for herself.' What was she doing? Molly thought. This had to be one of the most magnanimous gestures of her adult life. Angie had done the dirty on her. She didn't deserve help like this.

Nevertheless… 'What she needs is a hero on a white charger,' she told him. 'Or her wonderful Guy loaded with so many flowers that she's blanketed with them.'

'It seems a bit excessive,' he said cautiously, and Molly almost brained him with a leg of the froghouse.

'Fine, then. Be boring. See where that gets you.'

'You really think that would work?'

'I really think so.'

He sighed and spread his hands. 'I'll do it.'

'Great. Oh, and Guy?'

'Yes?'

'Try to let her think that it was all your idea—and if anyone in this room ever tells her it wasn't then I'll personally nail them to the floor by their toenails.'

'Um…right.'

She grinned and flipped the door open for him. 'Go for it, kid. James Bond to the rescue.'

'Oh, and Mr Bond…?' Jackson pushed himself to his feet and grinned at Guy, and then at Sam. 'Young Sam here is in his school uniform.' He addressed Sam, who'd been fiddling with the aluminium legs. 'Does wearing your uniform signify you should be in school, Sam?'

'I ought to be,' Sam told him truthfully. 'But it doesn't matter if I'm late 'cos I promised Molly I can still be a brain surgeon and Molly said it's National Frog Day.'

Not many men could take that on board as quickly as Jackson but he did it without a blink. 'National Frog Day?' An eyebrow quirked upward. 'Very original. But, Sam, brain surgery takes real application and you can't start too young. Do you have everything ready for school?'

'Yes,' Sam admitted, reluctantly. 'But we haven't finished the froghouse.'

'I'll finish the froghouse. Guy, how do you feel about giving Sam a ride to school on your way to rescue your damsel?'

'But—'

'You know,' he said gently, 'Molly has given you the means to do the rescuing. You do owe her.'

And Guy relented. Boring or not, he really was a very nice man. He sighed. 'Sure. Of course I can. That's fine, Sam. If it's okay with you.'

'That's great.' Jackson beamed at this very satisfactory outcome for all concerned and swung the door wide. 'Off you go, then, children. Drive carefully. Off to learn to be a brain surgeon and rescue maidens in distress. What better way to face the world?'

Which left Guy and Sam disappearing hopefully out through the door and Jackson firmly closing the door behind them.

And turning to face Molly.

# CHAPTER NINE

SILENCE.

The silence went on and on. Let the floor open up and swallow me, Molly pleaded to someone who obviously wasn't listening. How can I be stuck alone with *him*?

'Thank you for the froghouse,' she managed at last. 'But there's no need for you to stay.'

'On the contrary, there's every need. We're going out for lunch and we haven't finished building.'

'I can put it together myself.' She swallowed and fought for some dignity. 'Thank you for giving it to Sam. I'm sure he'll appreciate it.'

'And you won't?'

'Yes,' she snapped, abandoning dignity forthwith. 'You're putting it in front of the television. Great. I *like* watching a tank of frogs instead of television.'

'I knew you would.' He grinned. 'You look that sort of girl.'

'You have no idea of what sort of girl I am.'

'Now, that's where you're wrong,' he told her, his voice growing serious. 'Because I've got it figured.'

'I don't want to hear.'

But he was brooking no interruption, talking almost to himself. 'You're the sort of girl who'd drop everything when her nephew's orphaned—drop the life you love—come to a city that you hate. Put up with your nerdy cousin and put your life on hold...'

'For my nephew,' she snapped. 'And a great guardian I make, I don't think. I slept in today. I drank too much last

126

night and I didn't even get Sam to school on time. Social welfare would have a field-day.'

'So how many times have you drunk too much since Sam was orphaned?'

'Just last night.'

'Then stop the self-blame. Anyone could see you had an excuse last night. It doesn't take an Einstein to figure out what happened. Angela arrived, having broken off her engagement. You were keeping her company.' His mouth quirked in laughter. 'Berating men in general.' He looked at her, his eyes searching and seeing maybe more than she wanted him to. 'And now Angela bolts, leaving you to face the music, yet you do your best to repair her relationship. Her man's off to buy the city out of flowers...'

She let herself get distracted. 'Do you think he will?'

'If he doesn't, he's a fool. You've handed him his salvation on a platter—and, considering the fact that Angela did the dirty on you, I'd call it a very generous salvation at that.' He grinned and motioned to the sideboard. 'Pity about the keys.'

The keys! Molly's gaze swung to the sideboard, where he was pointing. Oh, for heaven's sake, Guy had left the keys behind.

'You saw! You let him go!'

'Let's just say I didn't think Angela should be let off scot-free...'

Silence again. Molly tried a glower but it didn't come off. He was smiling at her, and his smile was enough to unwoman her completely. It made her want to melt...

Melting was hardly appropriate.

'It's stupid,' she said inconsequentially, to no one in particular. 'It's not Angela I'm mad at. You're the one who's the rat.'

'*I'm* a rat?' Those mobile eyebrows rose. 'How can I be

a rat? I'm buying a farm from you, *and* I saved your job, *and* I brought you a froghouse.'

She took a deep breath, searching for the words, and in the end only three would do. 'You kissed me.'

There. The thing was said. It hung between them, a bald statement of fact with nowhere to go.

'I kissed you.' His smile faded. He eyed her warily and Molly thought—not for the first time—a scanty bath-wrap with moonbeams all over it was hardly the most dignified covering for the discussion she was having.

No matter. She forged on with resolution. 'Yes.'

'Does kissing you make me a rat?'

There was only one answer to that. 'When you're committed to another woman it does.'

He thought that through. The newspaper, he thought. Hell, she'd seen it.

Should he deny it? His gut instinct was to do just that, but then... Hadn't he and Cara agreed never to be in danger of love? So maybe it was safer to let Molly think he was involved elsewhere. Then he'd be protected from just what was threatening.

'You mean Cara?'

'Who else do you think I mean? How many significant women do you have?'

Silence. Then, 'You think I was being unfaithful?'

Here we go, Molly thought. This man's morals were about as divorced from hers as they could possibly be. He had no idea that he'd done anything remotely questionable. In his eyes Molly was a woman, therefore she was available to be kissed. It was as simple as that.

'We hardly forged a relationship,' he said, and she nodded, expecting little else.

'No.'

'Then what's the big deal?'

'Nothing.' She was glaring at him with every ounce of glare in her possession.

'So why are you mad?'

'Let's just say I feel sorry for Cara and leave it at that.'

More silence. It stretched on and on. Then, 'Are you intending to come to lunch in that?' with a polite motion to her bathrobe, and Molly glared some more.

'No!'

'Then may I suggest you get yourself dressed while I finish the froghouse?'

'I don't want to—'

'Come to lunch with me? I can see that.' His tone was polite now, businesslike and aloof. Nothing more. 'But there's no choice—for both of us. So I'd suggest you come down off your high horse, haul yourself back into business mode and come out to lunch. Now.'

And without another word he turned his attention back to construction, leaving Molly to react as she would.

After all, it had nothing to do with him.

Only it did.

Molly left him alone, thumping back to her bedroom and slamming the door behind her. Left to his own devices, Jackson manoeuvred the froghouse legs into position and started tightening screws. It was a fiddly job and required concentration.

And concentration was what he didn't have.

Had he started a relationship by kissing Molly?

The question didn't arise, he thought. Or it hadn't until now.

So what had happened?

Very little, he told himself. Molly was a beautiful and desirable woman. They'd shared a wonderful day. It had seemed right at the time so he'd kissed her. As simple as that.

130 A MILLIONAIRE FOR MOLLY

Only it wasn't.

Damn, it was how she made him feel…

He'd never felt this way before, he thought suddenly. He'd kissed many women but he hadn't known he could feel like this.

Like what?

As if she needed defending and he wanted to be the one who did the defending. As if he wanted to share in watching these crazy frogs jump around their tank—as long as Molly was by his side to share in the watching.

As if he wanted to kiss her again…

That was the nub of the matter.

But since Diane relationships were off the cards. Except for Cara. And the relationship he had with his half-sister was, of course, completely different. She of all people understood why he'd vowed never to fall in love with anyone again—but Cara was in Switzerland now, living her own life. She wouldn't appreciate him interfering in her affairs—playing the protective brother.

But if someone touched Molly…

The thought brought him up with a jolt. If he thought anyone was likely to lay a finger on Molly… Hurt her…

No. Not just hurt her.

It wasn't only a feeling of protectiveness that was consuming him. It was the thought of anyone else…any man…looking at her with desire. Because she was…

Whew! Where were his thoughts taking him?

The stupid froghouse leg wouldn't fit and he swore.

Get this tank up, get this lunch over and get out of here, he told himself harshly. You need to clear your head, and being around this woman—

*You* want *to be around this woman,* the other half of him argued.

You don't.

He was so confused. All he knew was that he made a very bad liar. He couldn't even lie to himself.

And Molly?

She was dressing herself in the most severe outfit she owned. Black, black and more black. And no make-up. Not a scrap.

What was she doing? She dressed and then stared into the mirror for a very long time.

'Anyone would think you were scared of Jackson Baird,' she told her reflection, and stared for a while longer.

Finally she gave a little nod and the corners of her mouth twitched into a grimace.

'Anyone would be exactly right.'

There was the small matter of completing the froghouse, but they'd run out of time.

'I think I must need a different sort of screwdriver,' Jackson confessed. 'These plans look like they're written in Swahili.' Then he checked out Molly's black trousers, black jacket and black shoes and his frown deepened in disapproval. 'Plus I was hoping for someone to help me lift it into place, but the only thing you look like lifting is a coffin.' His eyes raked her from head to toe, disapproval growing by the minute. 'I've seen pallbearers look more cheerful than you.'

She hmmphed at that. 'I'm dressed for business.'

'And the fact that I need a lift to get this tank on its legs...'

'Your four legs aren't together yet,' she pointed out. 'Plus I need time to think about where to put it. It can't stay in front of the television.'

'What about in front of the bar? Will that be a problem?'

She managed a sort-of smile. Her head was aching from

the night before, she was confused and tired, and the last thing she wanted to be thinking about was the bar. Or its contents. 'Only if Angela breaks up with another fiancé,' she said ruefully, and he smiled in sympathy.

'Not a big drinker, then, Miss Farr?'

'The bar's hardly been touched since my brother-in-law's death,' she told him, and then wished she hadn't as his eyes warmed with still more sympathy. The last thing she needed from this man was sympathy.

She didn't need anything from him at all.

But he was still in sympathy mode. 'You haven't thought of ripping the bar out? Of changing the apartment so it's more yours and Sam's rather than Sam's parents'?'

She thought that through but didn't understand. 'The froghouse is doing that.'

'No.' He considered, but he knew he was right. 'Sam's belongings may well have arrived when his parents were alive.' He let his gaze drift around the place, taking it in. 'All the photos here are of his parents and of Sam's life before their death. All the personal stuff. There's not a lot of Molly Farr in this place at all.'

'It's Sam's home.'

'It's your home, too.'

'Sam needs memories of his parents.' She bit her lip. 'Heaven knows they'll fade soon enough.'

'It's natural that they should,' he said gently. He crossed to a shelf where a row of trophies stood. Golf trophies and netball trophies and sailing trophies and junior chess tournament certificates. 'There's a whole family's achievements here—but where are yours?'

'I don't count.'

'You do count.' He frowned. 'For Sam, you count very much. When you were a kid what were you winning?'

'Not much.'

'Cow-riding competitions?'

That brought a reluctant chuckle. 'I wouldn't think so.'

'Then what?'

'Nothing.' She met his gaze and held it, but still his eyes probed. 'We're going to be late for lunch.'

'No. We have time. What?'

'I didn't...'

'There must be something. Some memory of childhood that means a lot to you? Something you achieved?'

She sighed and let herself think about it. 'I guess—knots?'

*'Knots?'* Whatever he'd been expecting it wasn't that.

'I talked my way into joining the boy scouts,' she told him. 'My first merit certificate was in knots and I caught the bug.' Her voice tailed off. Surely he couldn't be interested.

But it seemed he was. He was fascinated. A junior Molly as a Boy Scout. The idea was fascinating. He could see her now... 'So then what happened?'

'You don't want to know.'

'Try me.'

She hesitated, and then shrugged. Why not? It was ridiculous, but the man was a client, she told herself. So she should treat him as a client. It was her job to keep him happy. Up to a point.

'Just a minute, then.' And a moment later she was scrambling around the back of her wardrobe. Her personal stuff was shoved behind suitcases, abandoned to neglect—as she'd abandoned her old life.

If he was really interested... Frame after frame was stacked neatly in the dark. She lifted the top three and carried them out.

Here were her knots.

Every knot she knew was represented in these frames.

She'd tied them with care, with love and with increasing skill. Here were farm knots, shipping knots, plainly functional knots and fancy decorative ones. Every conceivable way to join two pieces of rope was displayed in these frames. They were labelled with names and often had a tiny history written underneath. She'd started her frames when she was nine years old and the last knot had been tied two weeks before her sister died.

They were part of the Molly that was.

She carried them out and handed them over to Jackson in silence—and why it felt as if she was handing over a piece of herself she didn't know. He took them from her and stared down at them for a long, long time. His eyes took in the care, the love and the knowledge.

'These are fantastic,' he told her, and she flushed.

'Yes, but they're part of a past life.'

'They're part of you, and Sam should see that.' He lifted the top one and set it up carefully behind the netball trophies. 'They should be hung. You should have a feature wall of them.'

She shook her head. 'I don't want to make Sam's life different.'

'Sam's life *is* different.'

'Not any more than I can help.'

He stood looking down at her for a moment, and then the corners of his mouth twitched into a smile that was almost self-mocking.

'You're quite a woman.'

That was a good one. 'Yeah. And you're quite a man. But now we need to go to lunch.'

'So we do,' he said slowly, but the way he was speaking made her think it wasn't just lunch he was thinking of. 'So we do.'

\* \* \*

Hannah Copeland was a bright little sparrow of a woman. She was knotted with age and arthritis but her eyes were still alive with intelligence. She met them in one of Sydney's most exclusive restaurants and proceeded to treat the place—and the staff—as if she owned it.

'We're in my usual alcove,' she told them. 'I come here every Monday, regardless. It's my personal contribution to improving the world's economy.'

'Very generous,' Molly said, and she chuckled.

'That's what I think, dear.' She peered up at Jackson. 'And you? You're as wealthy as Croesus. What do you do to contribute to the world's fast lane?'

'Buy expensive farms?' he said, and her lined face lit with laughter.

'Very good.' Her keen eyes narrowed. 'But I don't believe in sleeping money. Will you keep my farm running as it should be run? You don't just want it as a tax dodge, I hope?'

'It'd be a very expensive tax dodge,' Jackson told her, helping her into her seat with care.

'You never know these days.' She settled herself down and surveyed her guest with complacency. 'Isn't this nice?' Then she peered more closely at Molly and at her dour outfit. 'You're not in mourning are you, dear?'

'She's in business,' Jackson said dryly.

'And you don't mix business with pleasure?'

'Never,' Molly told them. She lifted the menu, looked at the prices and gulped. She was way out of her league here. And…mixing business with pleasure? Did that mean she couldn't savour this extraordinary selection?

'Did you have a nice time at my farm?' Hannah asked, and Molly smiled. That at least was easy.

'Yes, thank you.'

'Doreen tells me the three of you got on like a house on fire. You and Jackson and the little boy.'

'There's no relationship,' Molly told her hastily. 'I only met Jackson on Friday.'

'But you like each other?'

'We like each other,' Jackson said, and Molly stifled a protest. Okay. For the duration—and for the sale—they liked each other.

There was a lull while they ordered. Molly thought of what she was eating in terms of how many normal meals she could buy and was silently having kittens—but she didn't let on.

Hannah was still concentrating on Jackson when the entrees arrived, which was just as well. It let Molly concentrate on food. She intended to savour every gorgeous mouthful. Then…

'You're engaged?' Hannah demanded of Jackson, and he frowned while Molly forgot all about concentrating on food.

'Where did you hear that?'

'I read my papers, dear. Tell me about your Cara.'

The frown stayed. 'She's not *my* Cara.'

'So you're not engaged?'

'No,' he said flatly, and Molly dropped her knife.

'You're kidding!' she managed.

'I'm not kidding,' he told her, and smiled—and she dropped her knife all over again.

'I thought…'

'Cara and I are happy as we are,' he told Hannah, and Hannah blinked and then speared a prawn as if it was an enemy.

'I don't approve of that kind of relationship,' she said. 'I like marriages.'

'In my world marriages seldom last long.'

'Promises last,' she snapped. 'If you mean them. Have you made this Cara any promises?'

He concentrated on his food for a little. It was well worth concentrating on, Molly thought. Their prawns were coated in some sort of tempura batter, tasting vaguely of coconut and served with a dipping sauce of chilli and lime. The prawns tasted as if they'd been out of the sea all of two minutes. But still Jackson had all her attention. 'I think my relationships are my business,' he said eventually.

'I want my farm to go to good hands.'

'I understand that.'

'I don't need to sell.'

'I understand that, too.'

Whoops, thought Molly. There goes Trevor's commission. If he was here he'd have a heart attack.

'Miss Copeland,' she said carefully, feeling as if she was treading through minefields, 'you did say that there were only two conditions.'

'Did I say that?' Another prawn was speared and the old lady popped it into her mouth and glared at the two of them. 'Then I've changed my mind. I'm not signing this afternoon.'

'Can I ask why not?' Jackson was courtesy itself. He obviously didn't have to face Trevor, Molly thought. Uh, oh.

But Hannah was concentrating on the pair who'd own her farm. 'I want to meet this Cara.'

'It's me who's buying the farm,' Jackson said bluntly. 'Not Cara.'

'But she'll be living there,' Hannah told him. 'No?'

'Yes. Eventually.'

'And the papers say it's Cara who's interested in horses. *My* horses. My horses are included in the sale and I want to know who's buying them.'

'Fair enough.' Jackson nodded. 'But it'll be three weeks before I'm back in the country again.'

'And you'll bring this Cara with you?'

'If I can.'

'Find out,' the old lady snapped. 'These modern arrangements…' She snorted. She looked at Molly and her gimlet eyes bored right through her. 'Are you engaged? Or married?'

'Um…no.'

'And you don't have one of these fancy arrangements?'

'No.'

'But you do have your nephew. Doreen told me about him.' A moment's silence while she considered, then, 'You'll be needing a man, then. The boy needs a father.'

Molly gave a faint smile. 'I think we can manage without.' Her smile deepened. 'Men are impossible.'

'They are at that.' But Hannah didn't smile and her eyes didn't leave Molly's. 'I never married. Didn't see the point. Never met anyone who could make my heart slam against a brick wall. You ever met anyone like that?'

'I…no.'

'Liar,' Hannah said without rancour. 'I can read it in your face. You let everything out with a face like that.'

'Really?'

'Really. Some man has treated you like dirt. Am I right?'

'Hey, I'm not even buying your farm,' Molly told her.

'So mind my own business?' The old lady grinned. 'You get as old as I am without a family to concern you and the world's your business. You have a good heart, girl.' She looked more closely at Molly. 'This man here hasn't been messing with it, has he?'

'No!' Molly practically yelled. A hush had chosen just that moment to fall over the restaurant and her 'No' echoed out over the other diners. Heads turned. She blushed. 'Do you think we can get back to business?'

'No,' Hannah told her cheerfully. 'This lunch isn't about business. It's all about getting to know you.'

'Getting to know Jackson,' Molly corrected her, and Hannah sighed and smiled.

'Maybe. I haven't made my mind up yet.'

'Are you getting cold feet?'

With the main course over, Hannah took herself to the powder room, leaving Molly and Jackson together. To her surprise Jackson had decided to be cheerful about the inquisition. He'd answered Hannah's questions about his background, and more and more Molly found he was turning the tables on the old lady. Hannah had ended up talking about herself, and her love of her farm shone through.

'I'm not getting cold feet,' he told her. 'The more I hear about the farm the more I want it.'

'You know, I'd be surprised if Hannah lets go entirely. Doreen and Gregor may not be the only elderly retainers you're left with.'

'You think Hannah will visit?'

'If you make her welcome.'

Silence while he thought about it. Was he thinking he'd hate it—or that Cara would hate it? Molly didn't know. His face was impassive.

A shiver ran through her. He saw it and was instantly concerned. 'Cold?'

'No.' She shrugged. 'Nothing. A ghost walked over my grave.'

'Something's worrying you?'

'No.' But his concern made her want to shiver all over again. She did feel cold. Forlorn. Bereft. Which was utterly ridiculous.

Hadn't she sworn off all men for ever? So why did this man have the power to unnerve her?

'Molly…' He held out a hand across the table to her and she stared down at it. It was a gesture of comfort—nothing more. She should reach out to take it.

She couldn't. She sat and stared at the hand. His eyes met hers and held, but there was a message there that neither wanted to read. Or neither was brave enough to read. Slowly he withdrew his hand, and very carefully she tucked both her hands safely under the table.

'Thank you, but, no,' she said, and he hardly knew what she was refusing. Or did he?

Hell, he was in deep water here, and he hadn't even realised he'd been sliding right out of his depth.

The tension was broken by a yell.

'Molly!' The yell came from the far side of the restaurant. Molly swung around to find Hannah returning to their table—and Angela waving furiously from the restaurant entrance. Half the restaurant had swivelled to see.

Angela was still wearing her mini-skirt from this morning and her crazy stilettos, but she'd added Guy's pinstripe jacket for warmth. Her blonde curls were still tousled from sleep, she was waving wildly across at her friend and she looked like someone who'd come straight from a welfare sale.

Dear heaven…

This was never, ever going to be a professional sale, Molly thought despairingly, and closed her eyes—just for a millisecond—just to find enough courage to open them again. When she did, Jackson and Hannah were staring in open-mouthed astonishment at the vision weaving her way through the tables.

Angela was talking full throttle before she reached them. 'Molly, you'll never guess what's happened!'

'Don't tell me. Your wardrobe's been eaten by silverfish and you've lost every hairbrush you own.' Molly groaned. 'Angela, for heaven's sake—'

'Where's Guy?' Angela was hardly listening. 'Oh, heck, I've left him behind.' She searched backwards and found who she was looking for. Another cheery wave across the restaurant 'Guy. They're over here!'

Apart from his jacket Guy, thankfully, was staidly dressed, but it was a different Guy from the Guy they'd seen two hours ago. His beam was wide enough to split his face as he came up behind Angela.

'Great. I knew we'd find them here. I've heard on the grapevine Miss Copeland almost single-handedly keeps this restaurant afloat.'

'You're so clever.' As he arrived at the table Angela gave him a hug, and Guy hugged her right back. Molly could only stare. This time last week Guy would have been mortified to see Angela looking like this. This Guy seemed not even to notice

'We came to fetch Angela's keys,' Guy said, and Molly blinked. But at least she knew what was wanted.

'You left the keys on the sideboard at Molly's place,' Jackson said blandly, and Guy groaned.

'You didn't think to bring them with you to lunch?'

Jackson's blandness cracked, just a little, and there was a trace of laughter on his voice. 'We...er...we didn't think you'd come after us.' He swallowed his laughter. 'Miss Copeland, may I introduce Angela and Guy? Angela is another realtor, who works with Molly, and Guy is her...' He hesitated.

'Her fiancé,' Angela finished for him proudly, and beamed and beamed. She thrust out her ring finger and the diamond sparkled in all its glory. 'I wasn't for a while, but now I am again and this time it's for ever. Guy might have forgotten the keys but he didn't forget my ring.'

Molly cast a sideways glance at Hannah and found her beaming to match Angela. 'At last,' the old lady approved. 'A proper relationship. You don't want to buy my farm, do you, dears?'

'For three million?' Guy grinned and held his love tight. 'Sorry. No chance.'

'You know, realtors wear the strangest clothes,' Hannah said, perusing Angela from head to toe and wrinkling her already wrinkled nose. 'One dresses for a funeral and the other dresses for…'

'For passion,' Angela said promptly, and giggled again. And then she explained. 'Guy arrived with a bus,' she told Molly. 'A whole bus.' She hugged her beloved, who was turning a delicate shade of gratified pink. 'There was a florist just near the school, where he dropped Sam. He said there wasn't room in his car for all his flowers and there were kids lining up for a school excursion. So he made a practically obscene donation to their literacy programme— plus he shouted them all ice cream cones—on condition that they detoured past my place. He gave every kid on the bus a bunch of roses and they came up the fire stairs to deliver them.'

'Good grief!' Molly's eyes flew to Guy, whose pink was turning fast to crimson. Wow! The man had improvised on her suggestion and then some. She hadn't known he had it in him.

'I was standing on the landing with a really angry taxi driver, because I'd left my handbag at your place, and all these kids filed up and handed me their roses one after another. Then Guy got down on bended knee and asked me to marry him—and the kids were watching and cheering… What was a girl to do?'

'How…how special,' Molly said, and Angela beamed some more.

'It is.' She turned to Hannah, moving right on. 'So you're Miss Copeland.' She held out her hand in greeting. 'How do you do? Are you trying to shake some sense into these two?'

'Sense?' Hannah sounded totally bemused.

'These two are made for each other,' Angela declared. 'But he's engaged to this other woman—'

'Angela!' Molly was on her feet, enraged. 'You're way out of line!'

'He's not engaged,' Hannah said, and Molly thought, Please let the ground open up under me. Please let this be a nightmare.

'He's not?' Angela was brought up short. She focused on Jackson. 'You mean the woman in the newspaper is not your fiancée?'

He gave a wry smile—but he was watching Molly. What had Angela said? *These two are made for each other…*

'Um…no.'

'Thank heaven for that,' Angela said bluntly. 'Marry Molly.'

'Angela!'

'Oh, for heaven's sake…' Jackson was half-laughing, half-exasperated, but Molly was no such thing. She was just plain appalled.

But Hannah was listening intently. 'Do you think he should?'

'Yes,' Angie said promptly, and hugged her Guy close. 'She should be as happy as I am.'

'He's never going to marry her if she wears funeral clothes,' Hannah said, and Molly took a deep breath.

'Excuse me!'

She was ignored. 'She doesn't usually wear black,'

Angela explained. 'She usually looks gorgeous. Only her sister and brother-in-law were killed and she has to look after her little nephew—who's a real sweetie, but she feels totally responsible. She and her fiancé were saving for a house, but when Molly said she had to look after Sam the creep told her the wedding was off. And he had the whole deposit in his name—which is why the first rule of buying a house is don't trust anybody—and don't ask me why Molly trusted the creep, but there it is, and now he's got her money and she has nothing. And then...' She took her first breath for about three minutes and it was a long one. 'Along comes Jackson.'

'Jackson,' Hannah repeated faintly, and Angela pounced.

'She's nutty about him,' Angela declared, and Molly felt herself sliding under the table. She held onto the edge and managed to stay upright, but it was a near thing. '*And* he kissed her.'

*She's nutty about him...* Jackson turned to stare at Molly's blenched white face. Put that on the backburner, his brain told him. Concentrate on practicalities. 'How many people know that I kissed you?' he demanded, and Hannah chortled and answered for her.

'The entire restaurant, at least.' It wasn't an understatement. The whole restaurant had hushed to a deathly silence and Angela had the floor.

'Anyway, it's true.' Angela flushed slightly and sounded defensive, but still she continued. 'Molly came home after the weekend lit up like a Christmas candle, and it's the nicest thing that's happened to her since the loathsome Michael. And now there's this stupid newspaper article.' Her eyes narrowed on Jackson. 'But you're not engaged?'

'No! And I don't believe the paper did say I was engaged.'

'Then this Cara—'

'Is none of your business.' Jackson closed his eyes for a brief respite and then he rose. With resolution. Things were getting entirely out of hand and he wanted time to think.

'I need to go. Miss Copeland, if you're not prepared to sell me the property—'

'Oh, I am.' Hannah's eyes were alight with laughter. 'But not just yet.'

'I don't like being messed with.' He wasn't looking at Molly as he said it.

'Neither do I, dear.' Their eyes locked and Molly thought, She's as astute at business dealings as he is.

'Then what?'

'You're coming back from overseas in three weeks?'

'Yes.'

'Then I'll sign in three weeks,' she told him. 'Down at the farm. After I've met this Cara.'

'I...'

'That or nothing,' she told him. 'You do want to buy the property, don't you?'

He did. They could all see it. Part of him wanted to walk away from this deal—walk away from these crazy lady realtors and from emotions he didn't know how to handle. The other part knew he was getting a never-to-be-repeated bargain. The farm was indeed wonderful.

Common sense won. 'Yes,' he snapped. 'But I'll deal through my lawyer and no one else.'

Hannah nodded. 'But you and Cara will be there in person in three weeks—and I'll deal through Miss Farr and no one else.'

'I'm not going back to the farm,' Molly wailed, and the attention of the entire group swivelled to her. The attention of the entire restaurant swivelled to her.

'Of course you're going,' Hannah told her.

'And there's the little matter of releasing Sam's frog,' Angela added. 'What better reason to make another trip?'

That was enough to sidetrack Guy, if no one else. 'You're building a Taj Mahal of a froghouse and *you're going to let the frog go*?' Guy was incredulous.

'They won't breed in captivity.' Molly was distracted past the point where anything was making sense. She was grasping at straws.

'And breeding's important,' Hannah approved. 'Mating. Relationships. The whole gamut of—'

'Of frog life?' Jackson was standing gazing at the lot of them. 'I see.' He shook his head. 'Enough. I'm off.'

'Me, too,' Molly said, and picked up her handbag and headed for the door.

'You'll both be at the farm on Saturday three weeks from now?' Hannah demanded after he and Molly paused.

There was a long silence.

If she didn't go she wouldn't have a job, Molly thought.

And Jackson thought if he didn't go he wouldn't have the farm he so badly wanted.

'Yes,' said Molly.

'Fine,' said Jackson.

'Excellent,' Hannah told them both. 'And now I suggest we all settle down and have sweets. The lemon tart here has to be eaten to be believed.'

'I believe I've had enough,' Jackson retorted. His eyes swung to Angela. 'Tarts and all.' And he walked out through the door as if he was being shot from a cannon.

# CHAPTER TEN

IT WAS nine o'clock in the evening and Molly hadn't yet recovered from the disastrous 'business' lunch. Sam was asleep, but under protest. 'How can we have such a great froghouse and not finish it?' he'd demanded. 'Our frogs are only here for three more weeks. The way it's going we won't finish until it's time for them to leave.'

'Yes, we will,' Molly told him, staring in dismay at the instructions for frame assembly. Maybe they could just fill it up without putting it on legs, she thought. Maybe she could get Angela and Guy to stop thinking about each other for long enough to come over. Maybe she could figure it out herself.

Ha! None of those solutions was remotely possible.

'I'll ring the aquarium,' she told him as she tucked him in. 'They'll send someone over.' Though it'd cost her money she could ill afford.

'Mr Baird said he'd fix it.'

'Yeah, well, let me tell you something. Have you noticed how good-looking Mr Baird is?'

'Um…no.'

'Trust me. He's good-looking. And it's time you took on board some sage advice, young man. Never trust the good-looking ones.'

He thought that over and frowned. 'Girls, too?'

'Yes. Girls, too.' But mostly men, she thought. Mostly men.

'I really thought that he'd come,' Sam said sleepily into

his pillow. 'I'm sad that he's so good-looking he breaks promises.'

And so am I, Molly thought, back in the living room and staring at various construction bits. Really, really sad. And if I wasn't a girl with responsibilities I'd go find myself another tub of Tia Maria ice cream. She stared down at Sam's frogs, who stared back at her from their too-small box with expressions of mutual lack of interest.

'Okay. Okay. I'm useless as a builder but I make a great realtor. When I go to bed I'll let you guys free in the bathroom.' Then she thought back to something Jackson had said and an appalling possibility presented itself. 'Only you have to promise to leave the toilet alone. Even I don't think life's that bad.'

This statement didn't cheer the frogs up at all. Well, why should it? It certainly didn't cheer her up.

Bed...

The doorbell rang and she jumped a foot.

It'll be Trevor coming to haul me over the coals, she told herself. He'd been appalled that she hadn't finished lunch with a signed contract. She swung open the door with a sigh.

'I've come to fix your froghouse,' Jackson told her, and walked straight in.

To say she was shocked would be an understatement. 'You what?'

'I've come to fix your froghouse. Like I promised.'

She thought about that while he set his toolbox on the floor and rolled up the sleeves of his sweater—and somehow she made her voice work.

'You know...what went on at lunchtime...I sort of figured that might negate any promises.'

'I didn't promise *you*,' he told her brusquely. 'I promised *Sam*. And I've got the right gear now.' He set a man-sized toolbox on the floor and Molly stared down, stunned and impressed.

'Hey, nice outfit,' he told her, and she forgot about the toolbox and flushed scarlet. She was wearing rose-pink jogging pants and sweatshirt, both of which had seen better days.

'You're kidding.'

'Beats the funeral clothes.'

She glared and decided to concentrate on the toolbox. It seemed safer.

'Do you know how to use that stuff?'

'Sure I do.'

But there was something about the way he said it that defied belief. Her lips twitched, despite her shock. 'Why don't I believe that?'

'Hey…'

'What's this?' she demanded, picking up an implement of not so obvious destruction.

He looked superior. 'That's a router.' His tone was of such confidence that she didn't believe a word.

'What does it do?'

'It routs of course.' He grinned. 'Anything you want routed, I'm your man.'

Yeah, right. Drat the man. How could he unnerve her so completely and then make her want to laugh? She swallowed a giggle and tried to be serious. 'That's the biggest set of tools I've ever seen.'

'I knew you'd be impressed,' he told her. 'That's why I bought it.'

'You bought a set of tools—*just for tonight*?'

'There's lots to do tonight.'

He was looking lovely, she thought. Just lovely. In his faded old jeans and a soft cashmere sweater that looked lived in and loved, he didn't look like a millionaire businessman. Tonight he could be anyone, she thought. Anyone's boyfriend? Anyone's lover?

He wasn't. He was Jackson Baird, client, with his arrangement with an unknown Cara, and she'd better remember it.

'The froghouse shouldn't take too long,' she managed.

'Not with these tools. But then we need to hang your frames.'

'My frames?'

'Your knots.' He concentrated on his tools, fitting a fierce-looking blade into a screwdriver handle. 'I'm not going back to the States until I see your knots on the wall. I've decided you've been a doormat for long enough.'

She stared. 'I'm not a doormat.'

'Yes, you are. You sit back and let things happen to you. For instance, have you tried suing this Michael character for the money you put into your home?'

'Michael's a lawyer,' she told him stiffly. 'He could beat me hands down in a legal fight. And I'd have legal costs and he wouldn't.'

'That's what he's counting on. What if I lend you my Roger Francis? He should be nasty enough to take on any Michael.'

'I don't like—'

'You don't like Roger Francis?' He grinned. 'Neither do I, but the man's clever. I'll be willing to bet he could take on any Michael you like and expect to win. So the offer's there.'

'Why are you doing this?' she asked, and he shook his head.

'Beats me. Give me a hand with these legs.'

But the question still hung.

And it hung all that night. They worked side by side, erecting the froghouse and then filling it with water and standing it in all its glory against the bar. It meant you couldn't lean against the counter, but Molly didn't do a lot of bar-leaning anyway, and it was the most sensible place to put it. Then she watched as Jackson gently released two little frogs into their new home.

Drat the man; he still had the ability to make a lump form in her throat. He stood in his lovely casual clothes, with the two tiny frogs nestled in the palm of his hand, and he handled them with the care he might well use if they were diamonds.

More so.

Jackson was a frog prince, she thought inconsequentially. With those two little creatures in his hand he seemed transformed himself, from ruthless businessman into someone...

Someone she could love with all her heart and with all her soul.

She bit her lip, and Jackson looked up and saw the expression on her face.

'What?'

'Nothing.' The frogs wouldn't jump off his hand. Neither would she if she was a frog, she thought, and then thought, Whoa... She was being ridiculous.

With his spare fingers Jackson was tickling the frog's smooth backs. She watched as his index finger stroked each body in turn and her own body shivered. The whole scene was unimaginably, crazily erotic.

Oh, for heaven's sake! She should take a cold shower. She cast Jackson an angry look, which he fielded as if he hadn't seen it, then she reached in and moved the frogs from his palm to a mid-pool rock. Their fingers touched in the process. They stood side by side, staring down at the tank.

'Um... You can go now,' Molly said finally.

'Not until the knots are up.' Still he was watching the frogs. They sat side by side, gazing over their new home of waterfalls and ponds and lush green foliage, and Molly could almost swear they were grinning.

'They're set for life.' Molly gave Jackson a half-hearted smile. Wherever she looked there were problems, she thought, and another problem had just raised its ugly head. 'You've spent all this money and now... Guy's right. It's silly. When they go it'll be empty, and Sam—'

'Will miss them,' he finished for her. 'I've been meaning to talk to you about that.'

'You have?'

'I have.' He grinned. 'There's a brochure in the side of my toolbox labelled "Frog Rescue Society". Did you know that homeless frogs can be farmed out to foster parents until they can be released?'

He'd taken her breath away. 'You're kidding?'

'No. The foster parents can be anyone, as long as they're prepared to do a little study, practise their mosquito-catching and prove they'll be good carers.'

'You mean Sam and I could be foster parents?'

'You have the froghouse for it now,' he told her. 'I don't see why it can't be of use.'

He'd taken her breath away. 'Sam would love it.'

'I know,' he said, and tried to look modest, and she fell in love with him all over again.

But she had to stay businesslike! All she wanted to do was take his face in hers and kiss him to bits and *make him want her*...

She couldn't. He was leaving. He had another woman to love called Cara...

'You found all that out for Sam?' she said in a choking voice, and his modest look gave way to abashment.

'Yes. Just call me Mr Wonderful.' And then he relented.

'Actually, the guy in the aquarium place told me about the rescue society. He gave me the pamphlet. So caring for frogs could be an ongoing experience.'

It was just what Sam needed, Molly thought. A cause. He'd take it on board and he'd love it.

'Thank you.' It was lame, and she knew it, but she didn't trust herself to say anything else.

There was a drawn-out silence. He was watching her. She should say something else, but all she could think was, this man is leaving tomorrow and I'll see him once more in my life and that's it. *It.* And then—nothing.

Somehow she had to sound normal. Sane. Uninvolved, even. 'We'd better do these frames.'

'Right,' he said, but he was still looking at her.

'You don't have to,' she said stiffly, but he didn't say anything more. He just crossed to the toolbox and found hooks and hammer and headed for the far wall.

There was nothing else to be said between them. Was there?

An hour later she had a display wall of all her knots. Every conceivable knot. And it looked wonderful.

'What's that one for?' Jackson asked, pointing to an obscure knot under his thumb. 'The slingstone hitch?'

'Anchoring lobster pots,' she told him automatically. 'You can tie it at either the bight or the end. You pull the ends and the turns in the standing section are dropped into the loops.'

'Right,' he said faintly. 'What knowledge! Just like my routing.'

'Not like your routing at all,' she said severely, and he grinned.

'Fine.' He laid down his hammer and surveyed the wall with satisfaction. 'More than fine. Now the place isn't a relic of the past. It's moving into the future. You'll be able to discuss the slingstone hitch with anyone who comes along, regardless of whether they're for tying it at the bight or at the end.' His smile widened, holding her. Touching her without touching. 'You and Sam should be right now. With your frogs and your knots.'

'I…yes.' He was right, of course. She should have done this before. This made it home.

Almost.

Home was where the heart was. But where was her heart now?

'Would you like some coffee before you leave?'

He was looking at her strangely and she wanted him to stop it. Or did she? 'No. Thank you.'

'What's time's your flight tomorrow?' She was sounding like an inane fool but at least she was sounding. It was hard to make her voice work at all.

'Early.'

'Oh.'

'I should go, then.'

'Yes.'

They were so close. So close. She could reach out and touch him. Reach out and take him…

And then what? A one-night stand? More of Jackson being unfaithful to the unknown Cara?

She wasn't a one-night stand sort of girl, she thought numbly, and she looked up to find Jackson's eyes searching hers. She knew he was thinking exactly what she was thinking. Wanting what she was wanting.

'Molly…'

'Don't.' One more word and she'd fall blindly into his arms. He wasn't asking anything of her. He wasn't. But he just had to stand there and he was asking without words…

'Go.'

He looked at her for a long, long moment and then finally he nodded. As if a decision had been made but it hadn't been easy. 'Maybe it's just as well.'

'Yes,' she snapped, taut to breaking point. 'After all, there is Cara.'

'There is.'

'So you shouldn't even be here now. Or doesn't Cara mind you spending evenings with other women?'

Another moment passed. Then he caught himself, reached into a shirt pocket and produced a card. 'This is where you can find Roger Francis,' he told her, and his voice had switched suddenly back into formality. Business. 'He's expecting your call. By the time I come back I'd hope you'll have instigated legal proceedings against your Michael.'

'He's not *my* Michael.'

'Well, against your money.' He smiled and then put a finger under her chin, dragging her gaze up to meet his. 'I'm sorry, Molly.'

'Sorry?' She took a deep breath. 'Sorry for what?

'I think you know.' He shrugged and gave a derisory laugh. It was directed straight at himself. 'Sorry that I have nothing more to give.'

And he bent and kissed her—hard on the mouth—a swift, demanding kiss that asked no questions and required no response.

It was a kiss goodbye.

And then he was gone, striding along the corridor and out of sight. Gone.

# CHAPTER ELEVEN

'MOLLY?'

'Yes.' Sigh. 'What is it, Angela?'

There was a long pause as Angela absorbed the inflection in Molly's voice. 'Then you're really mad at me, right?'

'Let's just say relations are strained.'

'Because I was honest with Jackson? Oh, come on, Moll, give me a break. Did I do real damage? Was the guy going to fall for you if I hadn't stuffed it up?'

'No. Of course he wasn't.'

'There you go, then.'

'But telling the man we were made for each other was unfair.'

'I thought he should see things as they really are.'

'Thanks, Angie. I do have some pride.'

'My mum says pride and love don't go together.'

'No. Me and millionaires don't go together. Honestly, Angie, I could have crawled under the table!'

'You haven't heard from him?'

'Of course I haven't heard from him.'

'It would have been nice.'

'It would have been...ridiculous.'


'Cara?'

'Jackson. Lovely. Where are you, darling?'

'New York. Where I'm supposed to be. I thought you'd be here as well.'

'I meant to be.' She hesitated. 'But I've met this man...'

Silence. 'Someone special?' Jackson asked cautiously.

'It seems like it.' She gave a slightly embarrassed laugh. 'Now, you're not to laugh. I know I've always sworn off men. After our mother's tragic example…well, I was never interested. But Raoul is so different.'

'Raoul?'

'He's French, darling. And he's just lovely. He's everything our mother and your father wasn't. He…oh, I can't explain. It's just everything I sort of planned has flown out the window.'

Jackson sat down heavily on the desk chair. To say he was stunned was an understatement. His half-sister. In love.

'That's great,' he managed. 'Can I meet him?'

'I'm aching for you to meet him. Oh, Jackson, he's so special.'

She was lit up, he thought. She was…in love.

'I just wish… I just wish that dreadful Diane—'

'Cara, don't.'

'Yes, but I only had our appalling parents to get over. It's been so much worse for you,' she said bluntly. 'The parents were enough. Like you, I thought I could never marry—I never wanted to go down that road. But then along comes Raoul…'

'And sweeps you off your feet?'

'Well, yes.' She gave an embarrassed laugh. 'He's as different from any man I've ever met as he can be. Jackson, do you think you can possibly learn to forget Diane?'

'No!'

'Just because our mother and your father…'

'There's also Diane. I trusted her.'

'And she was out for your money.' Cara sighed. 'You were just lucky you discovered in time that the child wasn't yours. But you were so young, Jackson. There are some really nice people in the world. I hadn't realised. Just because we haven't met them until now…'

There were, Jackson thought. There was Molly.

But how the hell could he trust after what had happened to him? It was asking far too much.

'I guess this means you're not interested in settling in Australia?' he asked, pushing his thoughts firmly back to business.

'Well, no. It made sense to have a base when we didn't have anyone. But, Jackson, Raoul has an apartment in Paris and a property in the north of France. I don't think I need...'

'A half-brother?'

'I didn't mean that. I'll always want my brother.'

'But you'll want your Raoul more.'

'Yes. And I hope... Jackson, I so hope you can find someone. Jackson, I'm so happy.' He could feel her smile coming down the line. 'So—will you still buy the farm?'

He thought it through. There was still the farm. There was only the farm. 'Yes. If I can.'

'It's a great idea. Raoul and I intend to have children, so we can come and visit. And, hey, you can always leave it to your nieces and nephews in your will. After all, you can hardly leave your fortune to a lost dogs' home.'

How about a lost frogs' home? he thought inconsequentially.

And then he didn't know what to think at all.

Molly?

Maybe. Maybe he could...


'Molly? Are you okay?'

'Hi, Angie. Sure.'

'It was just you were so distant in the office today. Every time there weren't any clients you seemed to be out of the office. It seemed like you were avoiding me.'

Yeah. She was avoiding everyone.

'Is Sam okay?'

'Yes. He's fine.'

'Have you heard from Jackson?'

She let out her breath in anger. 'For heaven's sake, Angie, will you get off your soapbox? *Why* would I have heard from Jackson?' It had been a week. An interminable week.

'The man *is* buying a property from you.'

'He's dealing through his lawyer. He's only coming back to sign.'

'You're seeing his lawyer? The frog-squashing Roger? Oh, great. How cosy.'

'Angie, don't.'

'So I'm worrying about you. I have a right to worry about you. Stay away from Francis.'

'The man's offered to help me get some money back from Michael. Courtesy of Jackson.'

Silence. Then, 'So the lawyer's doing you a favour? I don't believe it.'

'Jackson's paying him,' Molly said quietly.

'But this is Michael we're talking of! Does Jackson's lawyer think he can get blood out of stone?'

'It's unlikely,' Molly admitted. 'At first I didn't want anything to do with it, but Mr Francis has convinced me that Michael has something to say.'

'Yeah. Like sorry, sorry, sorry. Don't trust him until you see the colour of his money.' She considered. 'Come to that, don't trust Roger Francis, either.'

'I don't trust either of them.'

'Then why do this?'

'I need the money for Sam.'

'You really think you might get it back?'

'I don't know what's going on,' Molly confessed. 'I'm as bewildered as you are. But it's Sam's future we're speaking of. At the moment I can't even afford to move him to a decent school. So I can listen.'

'But you won't trust.'

'No. I promise.'

'And you're accepting Jackson's help?'

'In this, yes. It seems sensible.'

'Well, at least that's something,' Angie conceded. 'The man owes you heaps.'

'How do you figure that out?'

'He broke your heart.'

'Michael broke my heart.'

'No. Michael broke your pride and your bank balance, but not your heart. You didn't look like this after you broke off with Michael,' Angie said.

'Like what?'

'Like...' Pause for thought, then, 'Like a hearth without a fire.'

That brought a reluctant chuckle. 'Oh, very poetic.'

'I read it somewhere,' Angie admitted. 'But it's apt. Molly, you must do something.'

'I am doing something. I'm working. I'm caring for Sam. I'm dealing with Jackson's lawyer to see if I can get some money back from Michael.'

'I mean about Jackson.'

'You already laid my heart on a plate for him. I don't know what else can be done.'

Angie had an answer for that. 'Get on a plane and go find him?'

'Oh, come on. Even you know that's a really stupid idea.'

'Yeah, well.' Angie retreated, baffled. 'Desperate times call for desperate measures. He who dares, wins. In for a penny, in for a pound.'

'Good grief. Where *do* you find this stuff?'

'I don't know.' Her friend gave a theatrical sigh. 'But the two of you—it all seemed so gorgeous.'

'Yeah. Me and a millionaire. And now it's me and a frog.'

That produced a reluctant chuckle. 'Have you tried kissing Lionel?'

'Oh, right. Now, if you don't mind... Go back to Guy, Angie. I do not need this.'


'Francis.' Jackson's voice was clipped and incisive. The only way to deal with his lawyer was clipped and incisive, he thought. Maybe he should find someone else to represent him in Australia—but at least Roger Francis was good at what he did.

'Mr Baird. How can I help you?'

'I was wondering whether you've been in contact yet with Molly Farr about the money she's owed.'

'I have that in hand.'

'You do?'

'I think it may work out very well.' The lawyer sounded sleek and self-satisfied, but then he always sounded sleek and self-satisfied. 'I found her ex-fiancé was having all sorts of conscience pangs about what he's done. In fact, he's preparing to fold his country legal practice and move to Sydney.'

'Why will that help Molly?'

'He's interested in a reconciliation.'

'You're kidding!' Jackson sounded stunned.

'He's finding that he's tired of country practice. He'd like a base in Sydney to start afresh, and if he reconciled with Miss Farr then he'd kill two birds with one stone.'

'Molly would never buy it.'

'It might be in Miss Farr's long-term interests to do just

that. After all, the man is a well-qualified lawyer with the potential to earn a great deal more than she could.'

'You mean you're advising her to reconcile for...for money?'

'I'm advising her to do what she thinks best. But the prospect of getting money out of the man by legal means is slim. Married to him—'

'No!'

'It is sensible.'

'No!'

Silence. Then a cautious, 'What would you like me to tell Miss Farr?'

Jackson was silenced. 'Nothing,' he conceded at last. 'It's none of my business.'

Another silence. Then, 'Do what you think best.' And Jackson slammed down the phone. Hard.


'Molly?'

'Michael! I have nothing to say to you.'

'No, don't hang up. We need to talk.'

'What on earth would we have to talk about?'

'About us.'

'There's no *us*.'

'There might be. Hell, Molly, I've been a fool.'

'Criminal, more like it. Anything you need to say to me can be said through Roger Francis.'

'But that's just it. He suggested we meet.'

'He did?'

'Yes. So I thought we could do lunch tomorrow, Molly. I'm paying. No strings attached. Just come and listen to what I have to say.'

'Give me one reason why I should.'

And he had the answer pat. 'Because Sam needs a family.'

'Oh, right.'

'Honestly, Molly, Roger Francis has spelled out just how much trouble you're in financially and I'm feeling dreadful about it. I never meant… Well, I never thought it through. And I didn't realise just how damnably I'd miss you. So I thought—'

'Hey, it was *you* who put me in trouble financially.'

'So I should help you out. And in the meantime…'

'In the meantime what?'

'Just come to lunch. Hear me out.'

'Fine, then. One lunch. And that's it,' Molly stated finally.

'Mr Baird, I'm ringing to let you know everything's running smoothly. The contract is ready for you to sign next week. Miss Copeland will be at the farm next Saturday, as will Miss Farr, and Miss Farr has the contract in hand.'

'That's fine, Francis. And will Sam be there?'

'Sam?'

'Molly's little nephew. Sam. If she's coming I'd like her to bring him as well.'

'Oh, right.' Roger sounded taken aback but amenable. 'You want me to tell her she's welcome to bring her nephew?'

'Yes. I want you to tell her she's welcome to bring her nephew.'

'Maybe she could bring her partner as well.'

'Her *partner*?'

'I believe things are going remarkably well between Miss Farr and her ex-fiancé. I saw him yesterday and he's very pleased. I suspect there's no need for legal action down that road at all.'

Jackson thought that through and he didn't like it. 'The man cheated her.'

'He's more than willing to reimburse her,' the lawyer said stiffly. 'I did think that your main aim was to get Miss Farr out of financial trouble.'

'Yes.'

'Then I believe I've succeeded. Her ex is a sharp-as-nails lawyer and he'll make a killing in the city. All he needs is a base and a trustworthy background. She'll provide that.'

'It's a sure thing?'

'She'd be a fool not to accept. And...' He hesitated. 'I believe there's a degree of fondness still there. Your intercession on her behalf may well have given the three of them the chance to form a family.'

'Fine.' Just great. So why did he suddenly feel ill? 'Was there something else?'

'No, sir. I'll see you next week, then. Down at the farm.'

'I wish I could say I was looking forward to it,' Jackson replied bitterly.


'Cara?'

'Jackson?'

'Cara, this love thing...'

'Mmm?'

'Cara, if your Raoul was engaged to be married to another woman—if you thought that engagement might be a disaster—would you just walk away?'

'Jackson...'

'What would you do, Cara?'

'We're not talking about Diane, here, I hope?'

'No. We're not talking about Diane.'

'Then who are we talking about?'

'Someone called Molly.'

'Is she special?'

'So special I won't stand in her way—if she's engaged to someone else and that's what she wants.'

'Are you sure she's engaged to someone else?'

'Maybe.'

'But you'll find out?'

'Yes.' He thought it through. 'I'll find out. And then I guess it's up to her.'

'Oh, Jackson...'

'Don't get your hopes up,' he said bleakly. 'Because I haven't.'


'Angela?'

'Molly?'

'Yeah. It's me. And I'm sorry it's so late...'

'Heck, it's one in the morning, Moll. What's wrong?'

'I think you need to come around. And I think you need to bring some more of that ice cream. And Tim Tams. A truckload of Tim Tams.'

'Um...any particular reason?'

'Yes. Because I don't know what the heck is going on and I don't know what on earth I'm going to do.'

# CHAPTER TWELVE

THE farm looked even more splendid than it had three weeks ago. Jackson's helicopter circled the boundaries to allow him to check every inch of his prospective purchase before landing. It really was the loveliest place on earth. All he had to do was talk Hannah around, sign a contract and it was his.

But why was he buying it?

Because it's paradise, he thought. But that wasn't a good enough reason. Not now. Could he use it?

I will, he told himself. I can work from here. With telecommuting and teleconferencing I can spend most of my time here.

*Yeah, with Mr and Mrs Gray—and a thousand frogs.*

And maybe with Molly.

And that was the crux of the deal, he thought. That was the half-formed desire. He just needed to see…

Hell, he should have more sense.

Isolation was what he did best, he told himself over and over. Had he learned nothing? Nannies and boarding school and distant parents were tools for survival. If he hadn't distanced himself from emotion—from any emotion—he would have gone under as a kid. His parents' love had come close to suffocating him and he hadn't been able to escape.

Then he'd made that one huge mistake. He'd fallen for Diane. He'd been young and he'd been foolish—and he'd let himself love. Or he'd thought he loved.

Then she was pregnant. 'Great,' he'd said, and he'd meant it. A family… For the first time in his life he'd conceded such a thing was possible, and the feelings he'd had for the unborn child had threatened to overwhelm him.

But a week before the wedding there'd been a note from someone warning him that he wasn't the father. *Say a name,* the note had said, *and see how Diane reacts.*

He shouldn't have done it. He should have trusted. But…

'Have you heard of…?' he'd asked—and all hell had broken loose. Stunned, he'd watched as the woman he'd thought he loved turned into a raging virago. How dared he question her? How dared he imply the baby wasn't his?

But he hadn't implied any such thing. All he'd said was the name.

The next morning she was gone. It had been a lying, cheating con, devised to steal money from a wealthy adolescent.

And that, with the history of his parents' failed relationship, had left him determinedly single for ever. Cara was the only person he trusted.

The farm was to have been a place where they could base themselves when life got tough. Now the farm would be only his, and the thought made him feel unbearably alone.

Which was stupid. After all, he'd constructed his life so he'd be happy alone. It had taken him thirty-three years to get this far—he didn't intend to regret it now.

But if Molly was here, waiting…

Molly would be with Michael.

Roger Francis had phoned just before Jackson left New York and told him they'd be arriving separately. Roger was driving himself, Miss Copeland was being driven by her chauffeur, and Molly and Sam and Michael were coming together.

Great!

Hell, he'd helped orchestrate her reconciliation with Michael, he thought savagely. He should be pleased.

He *was* pleased, he forced himself to decide. Sam would have a secure base. A secure family.

But with a man who'd been prepared to rob Molly blind...

It was none of his business! Hadn't he learned anything from the past?

He looked out of the chopper and saw the eager faces of Doreen and Gregor waiting to greet him. They were his future. No one else. With a sigh he summoned up a matching smile.

This was a great buy. He should get on with it.


'Michael, the road to Birraginbil's to the north. You should have turned off back there.'

'Are we going to Birraginbil?'

'Of course we are.'

'Look in the glove compartment, sweetheart. I have a surprise for you.'

'A surprise?'

'An engagement ring. And plans for a wedding.'


Things weren't going to plan.

Hannah Copeland was receiving in state, seated formally in the vast front parlour, and her displeasure was obvious the moment Jackson walked in.

'So you're alone,' she snapped. 'What have you done with your fiancée, young man?'

'I thought I told you,' he said quietly, crossing to shake her hand, 'Cara's not my fiancée.'

*Where was Molly?*

'Yes. But she's someone you have an arrangement with.'

'I *did* have an arrangement with her,' he said honestly, and watched her face. Her displeasure grew.

'You mean you haven't now?'

'No.'

'Can I ask why not?'

'I think that's my business.'

She rose, matriarchal in her annoyance. 'Then I'm not prepared to sell you my property. The arrangement was that I'd meet your intended.'

'I don't have an intended.' He spread his hands. 'There's only me.'

*Where the hell was Molly?*

He managed a smile and decided honesty was the best policy here. His precious privacy could take a back seat.

'Hannah, Cara is my half-sister,' he told her. 'She and I had arranged to share your farm, but she's fallen in love with a Frenchman. So I'm alone. I love this place, and I'm prepared to look after it as you'd want it looked after. But I can't give more than that. I can't claim relationships that won't happen.'

The old lady stared at him in bewilderment, and Jackson thought she could decide either way.

But then Roger Francis appeared at the door.

'What is it?' Clearly Hannah had no time for the smart lawyer and she was seriously displeased. 'Have you heard anything from Miss Farr?'

*'Where's Molly?'* For the first time Jackson voiced his thought. His brows clipped together. The agreement was

that she'd be here well before him. Hell, if she didn't even come…

'I'm sorry.' Roger Francis spread his hands in helpless anger. 'Of all the inept… Mr Baird, I can't tell you how sorry I am. I should never have let you look at this property in the first place.'

'What is it?'

'Your realtor has taken off for her honeymoon—taking your contract and your titles with her.'

Silence. The silence went on for so long that it became jarring. Miss Copeland stared her displeasure at both of them, and Roger Francis coughed and stole a glance out of the window, avoided looking at Jackson. As well he might. Jackson's face was stony and remote—like chiselled granite.

'What happened?' he asked at last, and Roger spoke again. Too fast.

'She rang from the airport a couple of hours ago. I tried to catch you before you left Sydney but your mobile must have been switched off. So now I have to tell you. The phone call was from your Miss Farr… She sounded giggly and apologetic and altogether too foolish for words. It seems this Michael arrived last night with tickets to Hayman Island for himself, Molly and the boy. And plans for their marriage. He wouldn't take no for an answer and, as she said, it's not often you get an offer like that. So they left.'

*So they left.*

'They were on the nine o'clock flight from Sydney.'

They'd almost passed in transit, Jackson thought, and he felt sick.

Why? Because of the farm?

No. He knew damned well that the farm didn't come into it at all.

'And what of the contracts?' Hannah demanded, but her eyes were on Jackson's face. She wasn't interested in contracts—or farms—either. There were undercurrents here that she'd have to be obtuse not to understand.

Roger Francis spread his hands. 'I have no idea what she's done with them. Neither has her boss. I phoned him just now. He was playing golf with no idea of what had happened, and the news hit him as hard as it's hit me. It seems she just dropped everything and went.'

More silence.

'That's that, then.' Hannah's voice was bleak and final. 'No contracts. No partner. No Miss Farr. It seems I can't sell you my farm even if I want to, Mr Baird. Maybe when we get back to Sydney we can—'

'I don't think we can.' Jackson raked his fingers through his thick black hair and closed his eyes. His voice was as bleak as midwinter. 'Hell.'

'I'm sorry,' Roger said, and Jackson opened his eyes again and focused on his lawyer.

'You say you spoke to her?'

'Yes.'

'And she sounded happy?'

'Yes, sir. Exceedingly happy.'

'Damn.' He swore. 'I should have…'

'But you didn't.' It was Hannah, looking at him with open curiosity and seeing where his mind was headed. 'How about a fast trip to Hayman Island?'

'I'd never make it in time. And if she loves the man…'

'But what if she loves *you*?' she suggested gently—and waited.

'I don't know.' He groaned. And then he caught himself.

After all, he'd been trained since birth to receive blows. To receive hurt. He knew how to handle it.

Withdrawal. It was the only way.

'I'm sorry for wasting your time, Miss Copeland,' he told her and his voice was now strictly formal. Back to business. The shield had been put up again and it wasn't about to be lightly put aside. 'But it seems the fault's not entirely mine. You've obviously chosen an extremely unreliable realtor to represent you.'

'You can say that again.' That was Roger Francis. He eyed his employer sideways. 'If you want a place that's just for yourself, then the Blue Mountain property is far superior,' he said smoothly. 'You know it appealed enormously before you heard about this place. It's only an hour's drive from Sydney. I spoke to the owners only yesterday and your option's still valid.'

'I bet it is.'

'I'd be happy to show it to you again. We could take the chopper right now. I could organise someone to fetch my car—'

'Enough.' Jackson spread his hands and stepped back. 'Enough. I need time to think.'

'I have the Blue Mountain brochure in my briefcase,' Roger said smoothly. 'Shall I tell the helicopter pilot you'd like to leave?'

'No. Yes!'

And then he paused.

There was the sound of a vehicle approaching from the main track. It was being driven far too fast, and by the sound of the engine the car had seen far too many days to be travelling at this speed.

All eyes were drawn to the French windows as a battered

and dusty sedan drew to a halt in a screech of brakes and a cloud of dust.

Out tumbled Molly. Closely followed by Angela and Guy and Sam.

'Are we too late? Has he gone?'

Molly burst into the room with her arms full of documents. Then, as she saw Jackson, she stopped dead.

He took one step towards her. She dropped the documents from nerveless fingers. They scattered over the floor and in less than a second she was being held in his arms— as if she'd never be released again.

After that there was chaos. Angela and Guy and Sam were all crowding into the door behind Molly. Sam was clutching his frog box as if his life depended on it. But his attention—all attention—was on Molly. Who was sobbing her heart out on Jackson's shoulder.

'What the…?'

It was all Jackson had to say.

'I never thought he'd do it.' Molly was talking through tears into the soft linen of his shirt and he had to stoop to hear. 'I thought he was just playing games, so I figured I'd go along with it to see what he was up to. I didn't think it'd get serious. And then he got really nasty and tried to hold me back and I had to fight him…'

'Whoa!' He held her at arm's length at that. There was an angry bruise spreading from under her eye to her chin. She looked dishevelled and tearful and angry—and altogether far, far too lovely. 'Slow down. What happened?'

'It was Michael,' Angela burst out from behind them. She pointed to the hapless Roger Francis. 'And this…this weed.'

All attention swung to Roger Francis. Who looked suddenly pallid. And smaller somehow.

'What—?'

But Angela was mid-tirade, accepting no interruptions. 'He rang Molly and said Michael wanted a reconciliation—but Molly didn't believe it for a minute. So then she wondered—why was he so pushy? And why was Michael so pushy as well? Then she figured, Hang on, they're practically the same age, and how many law schools are there in this state? So she did a search—and guess what? She discovered Roger and Michael were in the same year at the same university studying the same subjects.'

'Which doesn't mean anything,' Roger said, but he was edging towards the door.

Molly had recovered enough to take over. 'And then Michael arrived and he was so nice.' Her voice was faltering but she was managing to put in her bit. Something about the way Jackson's arms were holding her was feeding her strength by the minute. 'I smelled the biggest rat. But he plied me with dinners and he gave Sam gifts.'

'Nothing as cool as the froghouse,' Sam volunteered, and Molly managed a smile.

'No. Silly, over-the-top presents. And the more Michael schmoozed up to us the more suspicious I got. And then he practically insisted he bring me down here today.'

'And he's got a nice car, and Molly hasn't got a car at all, and she didn't want to ask for a ride in your helicopter. Which I thought was stupid,' Sam said scornfully. 'You would have brought us—wouldn't you Mr Baird?'

'Yes,' he said promptly, and his hands tightened on Molly's waist. She looked up at his face with an expression that said she couldn't quite believe what was happening.

*Where was Cara?* she thought frantically.

Concentrate on the story. Not on the body against hers. Not on the eyes looking down at her, full of concern…

Only she knew the sheer effort of will it took to continue. To stop herself sinking into his embrace as if she'd never let go. But they were all still confused and she had to explain. Somehow.

'I didn't have a clue what was happening, but I talked it over with Angela and we decided the only thing to do was go along with him. So we duplicated the contracts and—'

'You duplicated the contracts?' Roger Francis's face was reflecting pure shock.

'Of course. I'm not stupid. So Angela had the duplicate papers ready with instructions to get them down here today if anything happened, no matter what. We even had Guy and his car on standby. Though…' She gave a rueful smile. 'We hadn't quite counted on Guy trading his sedan for honeymoon tickets and a car older than he is. No matter.' She hauled herself back to the matter in hand. 'Then Michael arrived.'

'And instead of bringing us here Michael took us to the airport,' Sam said, incensed. 'He said he was taking us on a holiday to Hayman Island.'

'It was the whole sweeping-me-off-my-feet routine,' Molly said grimly, and turned within the circle of Jackson's arms to stare at Roger Francis. 'You must think I'm really, really dumb.'

'Some girls would have accepted,' Angela said blithely. She and Guy had moved as one to block the door, leaving the hapless Roger no escape. 'Michael's a good-looking man and he was offering the holiday of a lifetime. And marriage…'

'As if I'd believe him.'

'He thought you were still in love with him.'

'How could I be in love with him when I...?' She faltered, and Jackson's arm tightened even further. The gesture had stopped being a gesture of comfort. It was a gesture of pure joy.

But Jackson was looking at her face and, joy or not, his expression was grim. 'So what happened?'

'So when he turned off the highway into the airport I told him he had to be joking. And he said don't be a little fool. He said...' She paused and then met Roger Francis's look head-on. There was hatred coming from him. Blinding, unadulterated hatred. 'He said we stood to make heaps from the commission on the Blue Mountain property. He said Roger was a part-owner. He was set to make a mint if the sale to you went ahead, and if that happened then we'd get a cut. He said before you saw this place you'd almost bought the other property and if this sale fell through—which it would if I messed them around and made both you and Hannah angry—then we'd all be laughing.'

'You'd be laughing? Married to Michael in Hayman Island?'

'I'm not completely daft.' She took a deep breath. 'He couldn't even get that right. He flashed the tickets at me as if that'd make it just great—but they were singles! He didn't even think I'd read the fine print—just blindly take him on trust. As if! He had every intention of taking Sam and me to Hayman Island and dumping us there.'

'You're kidding!'

'By this time we were in the airport car park. And I told him where he could put his tickets. When he told me not to be stupid, I grabbed Sam and started to leave. Then he took the contracts and tore them up. And he hit me.'

She'd been hit!

Jackson turned her then, twisting her in his hold so he could examine the bright angry bruise. And he uttered an expletive that made Molly catch her breath.

'Yes,' she said, but she wasn't upset by the bruise. The tone in her voice was one of satisfaction. 'But it did achieve one useful purpose.'

'Which was?'

'You don't think I'd let him hit me and get away with it, do you? Do you have any idea how much security there is at airports these days?'

'Well—'

'I screamed,' Molly carried on, considering his answer inconsequential. 'There were loads of people about, and I screamed the place down. My nose started to bleed, which was terrific. It's wonderful what a bit of blood can do for a drama. And then Sam head-butted him. He went to slap Sam and suddenly there were four hefty security guards holding him down and any number of witnesses. Plus a security camera. We've had him arrested.'

Her voice was suddenly almost joyous. 'He's in jail right now. Sure, he'll get bail, but I have heaps of witnesses, and the police say if I press charges I'll certainly get a conviction. Plus damages.' Her hand touched her cheek. 'For any amount of emotional trauma.'

'You're not emotionally traumatised at all,' Jackson said on a note of discovery, and she chuckled and, just naturally, her arms came around and hugged him back.

'No. I'm just very, very pleased that finally Michael has blotted his too-perfect copybook. There's a whole bunch of stuff a lawyer can't do once he has a conviction, and I can't wait to get it in place.' Then she lifted her chin and stared at Roger. 'So Guy and Angela brought us down here— *ventre à terre,* as the saying goes—which was very exciting, wasn't it, Sam? And now... I don't know how we'll deal with you, Roger, but Guy seems to think it's illegal to try to sell your client something without disclosing ownership. We might just get you, too.'

And Roger was stuttering. 'I don't... I haven't... The girl's...'

'Get out,' Jackson said grimly. He was staring at Roger as if he was some sort of pond scum. 'Get out!'

'I never—'

'You organised your thug to hurt Molly!'

And that was the nub of the matter. Everything else— the lies—the deception—they were things that would make him angry, but not to the point of white-hot fury. He looked down at Molly's face and he wanted to kill someone. The problem was there was only this weaselly little man in front of him to be killed.

But there were better ways of punishing than murder. So, with what seemed an almost supernatural effort, he stopped himself from picking Roger Francis up by the shoulders and heaving him through the French windows and made his voice cool, controlled and icy calm.

'Get out, Francis.'

'I can explain. She's mistaken. For heaven's sake...'

'You told me Molly was leaving for Hayman Island. You told me you spoke to her. There's no explanation other than that you were acting in collusion. Miss Copeland...' He turned to Hannah. 'Will you be willing to back me up as witness?'

'I surely would.' Hannah was staring at Francis as if he was some particularly repugnant insect. 'I'd be delighted. Hanging's too good for the likes of him.'

'It might not come to that, but what will happen will be

effective for all that. I'll see you in court, Francis. Now get out.'

'But—'

'Now!'

For a minute after the lawyer left there was silence. They listened as he gunned his car into action and headed off down the track, and they waited until the sounds of his car died to silence. Then Molly made to pull herself away from Jackson's arms, but was promptly pulled back again.

'Where do you think you're going?'

'I...um.' She thought about it and came to a fast decision. 'Nowhere?'

'Dead right. Nowhere.'

She liked masterful men, she decided happily. Okay, Michael had been masterful—*'Here are tickets to Hayman Island and you're coming with me!'*—but there was masterful and masterful.

This masterful was just plain wonderful.

'Thank you for bringing her down.' Jackson was speaking to Angela and Guy, but Molly was absorbing the soft texture of his shirt. Nice. And the feel of his heartbeat. Nicer still.

'Think nothing of it.' Guy waved an airy hand. 'The fact that my car blew a gasket or six and Angela and I missed a perfectly good day in bed—'

'Guy!' Angela gasped, but Guy only grinned. 'Well, we did.'

'I'll give you a decent car for a wedding present,' Jackson told them, and Angela rolled her eyes.

'Wow. That'll look good beside the casseroles and toasters.'

But Molly had hauled back, stunned. 'Jackson Baird, do

you think you can just splash your money about in that obscene—?'

'Hey, who's complaining?' Angela interrupted. 'Let him splash all he wants.' Her eyes were brimming with laughter. 'What about putting diamonds on the shopping list while you're at it?'

Molly caught her breath. 'Angie—'

'Don't tell me. You were about to say shut up.' She held her hands up in laughing protest. 'Okay. I know when I'm butting into something that doesn't concern me.' Angela looked down at Sam. 'Sam, the Lionels have been in that box for far too long.'

'They have,' Sam agreed.

'Then let's show them to their new home.' She took Guy's hand and Sam's hand and smiled at Hannah. 'How about it, Miss Copeland? Would you like to see a frog launch and leave these two alone?'

'I'd be delighted,' Hannah said, and tossed aside her walking stick. 'If what I think is about to happen *is* about to happen then I'm about to sell my farm. And if I'm selling this place then I want to leave a healthy frog population behind. Lead on, young Sam.'

'Hey, I'd like to see the frog launch too,' Molly said, stung.

'You want to see a frog launch or you want to spend a bit more time right where you are?' Angie demanded. 'Choose now. Frog or prince? What'll it be?'

And there was only one decision to make after all.

'Prince, please,' Molly said, and sealed her fate right there.


Then, finally, they were alone. Together. Standing locked in each other's arms. So much had to be said, but now wasn't the time for its saying. There was only time for each other. The feel of each other's bodies. Two hearts beating as one.

It was a joining without words. It was a feeling of such blessed peace—of rightness—of joy—that Molly could scarcely take it in.

Jackson was holding her to him as if he would never let her go. His hands were softly stroking the small of her back. Her aching face was leaning against his shoulder and his fingers came up to trace it through the tumble of her bright curls.

This was right.

This was for ever.

'Where's Cara?' Molly whispered at some point, but it no longer mattered. Cara no longer mattered. What true love had joined let no man put asunder—and true love had joined this pair as truly as any wedding vow.

He thought about that for a while. 'Cara and I decided living together at the farm would be crazy.'

She pulled away from him then, wanting to see his face. Wanting to understand. 'Why?'

He smiled down at her with an expression on his face that made her heart do handsprings. Oh, the joy of it. The pure, blessed joy.

'I've been a fool.'

'I don't believe you.'

'Then you wouldn't believe wrong. Molly...' He took her hands in his and searched for the words to explain something that he was only starting to understand now. 'Molly, I had the pits of a childhood. The only way I could be at peace was to institutionalise myself. Nannies. Boarding school. University and corporate life. Those things followed rules that I could understand. They made me safe.

So I tried to organise my personal life along the same lines. Cara is my half-sister. She lived the same bitter life as I did, with the same results whenever we showed emotional need. So when life got too tough—well, we were all we had.'

'Cara is your…*half-sister*?' Molly drew back, stunned.

'Yes. And until now Cara and I have been living under the same rule. Which is self-protection at all costs. I tried to move outside the rules once and it was a disaster.' He moved his lips in her hair and sighed, a great sigh. The sigh of a man reaching home. 'I thought I loved someone. She wanted me only for my money. I was young and stupid—but it made me distrust for life. Only then I hadn't met you. A man can be a fool…'

She could scarcely believe what she was hearing. Please…

It was a desperate little prayer, starting deep in her heart, but by the feel of his hands holding her close—by the feel of his heartbeat under hers—it had already been answered. 'But now?'

There was a kookaburra laughing outside, its raucous cackle making a mockery of the two lovers. But they didn't care. It could just as well be a nightingale, Molly thought, and found she wanted to pinch herself to wake up. She didn't need to. He was real and he was hers, and his next words confirmed it. 'But now Cara's met her Raoul. And…'

'And?' The whole world was holding its breath. Well, maybe not the whole world. There was one stupid kookaburra—but surely he didn't count.

'And now I've met my Molly. My love. My wonderful brave, funny, loyal, tender, wonderful Molly, and now I realise that I didn't know what the hell I was running from.

I thought I was running from love, but until I met you I didn't know what love was. We've spent three weeks apart and every moment I've missed you. I've ached for you. I've wanted you. Molly, I want you to be my wife. For now. For always. Will you marry me?'

*Will you marry me?*

The kookaburra was definitely a nightingale, Molly thought deliriously. She'd have it renamed by deed poll.

Would she marry him? Yes and yes and *yes*!

But there was one last thing. She had to say it, even though her entire future—her entire happiness—rested on it.

'Jackson—wherever I go. I need to take Sam. I…he's part of me. I must…'

But it seemed that Sam was no problem at all. 'Of course he is. How could I expect otherwise? He's the best kid, and I have such plans…'

'You have such plans?'

'We'll move here.' He put a finger on her lips and shushed her as she tried to speak. 'No, listen. You wanted things not to change for Sam, so you moved to the city. But things *have* changed for Sam, like it or not. I reckon he could be gloriously happy right here. The local school has to be smaller and happier than the one he's in now. He'll be able to breed frogs. He'll have his own pup and help breed cattle, and he'll eat Mrs Gray's pavlovas so he stops looking such a waif…'

'Oh, stop.' She was half-laughing, half-crying. 'You make it sound so wonderful. You make me want to agree just for Sam.'

'You think I'd blackmail you?'

'No.' She looked lovingly up into his eyes and then

laughed and changed her mind. 'Yes! If you want your own way, that is. You'll do whatever it takes.'

'I only want you.'

She held him still, their hands linked, forming a perfect circle of trust and of joy.

'Really, Jackson?'

'Really.' He bent forward and kissed her ever so lightly on the mouth. A feather kiss. A kiss of promise. A kiss of joy to come.

'And I've sorted it all out.'

'You have been busy.'

'It's a long time, three weeks. A man does a lot of thinking—of hoping—in three weeks.'

'So what have you decided?' They were making love with their eyes.

'I thought…I don't have to travel so much. I can mostly work from here. We'd be proper farmers. But, if you like, you could set up an exclusive farm sales agency. Only the best…'

She was laughing. 'Of course only the best.'

'And in our spare time we could be farmers together.'

'Yeah?'

'Yeah.' His eyes caressed her, but there was still a hint of anxiety behind them. An anxiety she loved. He was her big handsome prince who could rule the world. But when it came to his love for her he was putty in her hands.

She loved him so much she could hardly speak. And in the end she didn't have to. There was no need.

She placed her hands on either side of his face and she drew him down to her. Down to be kissed and kissed and kissed again. Kissed until they were both breathless with love and laughter, and with pure, unadulterated happiness.

And finally when they drew away—for an instant only—

Molly found the voice to whisper, 'We should go down to help release the frogs.'

'You've released your frog,' Jackson growled, and hauled her ruthlessly into his arms for yet another crushing kiss. 'He's your lover for life—and kiss all you like; he's never going to be a frog again.'

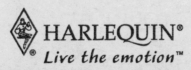

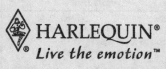

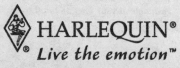